"Suck on that butt-hole!"

With all my love—

Bill

12/88

AUSSIE HOT

AUSSIE HOT

more homosexual experiences from Down Under

RUSTY WINTER

LEYLAND PUBLICATIONS
San Francisco

AUSSIE HOT IS COPYRIGHT © 1988
BY ROSS (RUSTY) WINTER

FIRST EDITION

ALL RIGHTS RESERVED.
Except for brief passages quoted in a newspaper, magazine, radio, or television review, no part of this book may be reproduced in any form or by any means, electronic or mechanical, including photocopying and recording, or by any information and retrieval system, without permission in writing from the publisher.

Front cover photo: © 1988 by P. Shane White
Reprinted with permission
Cover design: Timothy Lewis

ISBN 0-943595-13-4

A complete catalogue of books
is available for $1 ppd. from
LEYLAND PUBLICATIONS
P.O. BOX 40397
SAN FRANCISCO, CA 94140

Contents

First Light

I WATCHED THE LIGHT CHANGE from bluish-gray to gold. Early morning light. Glowing yellow. It spilled into the room of fading shadows and uncertain memories, forming a shapeless pool on the floor. In the room where I had been born and where my mother had died. The pool of melting butter oozed across the dusty floorboards as a gust of air gently lifted the layers of tattered fabric that hung over the window. I remembered my mother standing on a chair, the day before my tenth birthday, tacking the printed cotton bedsheet to the window frame "to pretty the place up a bit, dear." Six years ago. The year she went away. The cloth was colorless and worn now, and blotched with stains. It bulged inward with the motion of a billowing sail, filled by the warm morning breeze.

The sun would rise soon, but the new day already had heat. My body was hot and sticky. The pores of my skin opened to the moving air, taking it in, breathing. We slept naked on the narrow bed with no need of a sheet to cover us. He was lying flat on his back, leaving me almost no room. My neck was in the crook of his elbow, his right thigh between both of mine, and the air trapped in the hollows and valleys formed by our bodies was heavy with the odor of sweat, tobacco and sex. My body ached from forced stillness.

The pool of light on the floor expanded, flowing outward to touch the leg of the chair and then receded, as though liquid had soaked into the wood grain and dried. I looked at his head on the pillow. The curve of the full mouth, gaping. I looked at the sun-bleached hairs on his forearm across my shoulder, the pointed brown nipple near my mouth. I breathed in the smell of his damp skin. My body ached, but I did not dare shift or try to rearrange myself for fear of disturbing him. For fear of losing my own private landscape.

For several minutes the swathes of yellowed fabric at the window hung limp and still. But then floated inward once more, filling with air, forming an immense ballooning shape that trembled with mysterious life and occupied the room. I listened to day begin outside the room. The dawn chorus of birds: finches and wrens conversing in crisp whispers in the lilac bushes close by the window, currawongs and magpies more loquacious less near, painted parakeets, lorikeets and galahs shrieking stridently in the blue gums that fringed the home paddock. My mother's dressing-table mirror shone dully with reflections of night fading. The chair she once stood upon was standing at an odd angle, draped with yesterday's clothes, their inside seams showing. His clothes and mine.

The light was growing more intense beyond the curve of his shoulder. I wondered how he could sleep so soundly through the shrill cacophony of birds. I raised my arm cautiously to lightly finger the tangle of straw-colored tufts at his ear. They sprang back into position under my touch. I remembered watching my mother cut his hair with her sewing scissors; his fleshy, handsome face creased with laughter at her chiding because he would not keep still. (I cut his hair now and he laughs as he did then, still not keeping still.) I remembered, with my fingers at his ear, asking my mother why they called him Curly when there was not a curl on his head. She did not know why. Why she had not married him, I asked her that, too. She knew why, but her careful explaining had no meaning for my child's ears. Not then.

The light had crossed the floor to the far end of the room, creeping up the base of the old mahogany wardrobe. My eyes lingered on the familiar markings ingrained in the wood. Outside a rooster was crowing. The finches and wrens had moved away from the bushes by the window, and for a while I listened to the faint rustlings of the lilac leaves stirring against the fine wire screen. His head on the pillow looked large. I noticed a tremor under his eyelids and his lips quivered and twitched as though he might say something. I held myself still but my leg jerked, caught by a sudden cramp. Disturbed now, his body shifted, changed position, and under his displaced weight the thin mattress heaved and bedsprings creaked. I was enclosed by him, the shadow of his body cutting off the light. Wisps of his hair tickled my face, stubby bristles scraped my cheek, his breath was warm on my neck and more warm pungent air came from the moist hollows of his body. Air I breathed in, gladly. I could feel his heart beat, his sleeping breath-sounds were in my ear, a slight rasping or hitch in his throat. I shook my leg and my numb limb tingled as blood began to flow. Beyond the bulk of his body I could see light from the window brightening the room.

I do not remember how old I was when my mother told me that Curly was not my father, not even her lawful husband; though others did not know that. I remember we watched the sun set while seated on the steps of the narrow veranda. Dark pink and purple ribbons in the sky were drawn, like a conjuror's silk scarves, through a bank of pale lavender clouds. Curly was an orphan, raised in a state home for boys in Queensland, she told me. He grew up to be a skilled horseman and came to New South Wales, here, to the sheep station, looking for work. His skills and promise were recognized by the grazier and he was employed as a jackeroo. He was eighteen when they met; he, a fine strapping lad; and she, nineteen with a two-year-old child. She was a salesgirl in a nearby town when Curly came shopping for something—for what she could not recall, only that his was the most handsome face she had ever seen, the bluest of blue eyes—and one thing led to another. When I asked, my mother told me my father, a boy her own age then, had left her without a word, simply vanished, the day I was born.

The light grew more intense, outlining the sweep of his back, its deep curve to his buttocks. He opened his eyes. For a moment he looked at me as though I was a stranger to him, an intruder in his bed. Were his glazed eyes expecting to see someone else? The dark rings around his irises faded as he woke. I looked at him, and he smiled recognition. His face, close to mine on the pillow, drew back to look at me whole. He ran his rough hand down the skin of my back, his fingers finding the jutting bones of my spine, applying pressure, singling out each hard nub in turn like keys of an instrument. My mouth was dry, tasting of him. I wet my lips with my tongue and he traced the tip of his finger down the length of my nose and across my mouth. I caught him between my teeth, trapping him, and with my mouth closed began to suck, circling his finger with my tongue. He pressed his face into the curve of my neck, nuzzling, nibbling, sending little shivers to my groin. Then, pulling back, he gently held my head, lifted it between his hands like a drinking vessel, raising it to quench his thirst. Our lips touched. I felt the longing sigh of need reverberate in his body against mine. Breathless, he released his hold and lowered my head to the pillow. His steel-blue eyes glittered with diamonds of light and lust.

When my mother died I was left alone to live with Curly in his little house on the sheep station. The rules changed, and most disappeared completely. Curly never cared how late I stayed up and many nights I fell asleep slumped over my homework at the kitchen table. On these occasions he would gather me up in his powerful arms and carry me to the living room where I slept in a small fold-away bed. Straining to be quiet and gentle, he would undress me and tuck me in.

I do not remember exactly when I was aware that my falling asleep at the kitchen table each night had become a deliberate ritual. With my head cushioned on my arm I would wait, heart pounding, for the strength and warmth of his hands on my body. Being tenderly handled, being touched so lovingly by him had a half-conscious, dream quality of growing sensual pleasure. I would almost choke with horror and amazement as Curly's big hands undressed me and his fingers touched me everywhere, then lingered, feather light, at my crotch.

Nor do I remember when Curly realized that I was feigning sleep at the table every night. At some stage, as I matured physically, it became apparent that his not-so-casual caresses, his intimate exploration of my naked body, were responsible for my sexual arousal as well as his own. Not necessarily wanting to know but unable to resist, one night he found out what he needed to know. After undressing me as usual, he placed a quick deft hand between my legs where the fondling, the flutter of questing fingers sent ripples of wonder and delight through my limbs. I presented him with an immediate erection which he manipulated purposefully, proceeding with a delicate but determined stroking. I trembled with passion and, unable to stifle a cry, ejaculated into his gently pumping hand. He kissed my lips, loosely parted, as I gasped for air. He kissed my eyes that streamed with tears of joy and lost innocence. From that night on he carried me, sleeping or not, not to my makeshift cot in the living room, but to the bedroom, to his bed.

Light washed the walls of the room, gleamed in my mother's dressing-table mirror. I closed my eyes and shivered as cooling air rushed down one side of my body. The other half was hot against him. Turning my head, my lips brushed a part of him close by, skin that was weathered bronze yet remarkably soft. He propped himself up on his elbow to watch my face, but when I opened my eyes I saw him through a tangle of my own flaxen hair, luminous at the edges. Reaching, he pulled back a strand caught in the corner of my mouth. The light was blocked out by the mass of his head above mine. I thought I saw a sparkling of tears in his eyes, but with the light behind his head, I was not sure.

Curly's mouth found mine, greedily, and the weight of his body presed down with a gravity and urgency it did not have before. His mouth tasted of dry straw and semen. Our tongues probed, feeling each other like bloated slugs with rough and slimy skins. His evaporating saliva cooled the soreness of my lips, rubbed raw by his stubble, his hungry kisses. He rolled on top of me, flattening me to the mattress, mumbling endearments, his legs parting mine. I wriggled my toes playfully and slid my curled instep up the hard hairy incline of his left shin. I giggled a little, self-consciously, and wriggled my hips. His cock moved lasciviously on my belly. I sensed its need to be inside me. Drawing up my knees, I raised my thighs and wrapped my legs around his waist, crossing them at the ankles, anxious to be penetrated, to satisfy his need. Anxious to satisfy my need to have him inside me. Lulled into a feeling of supplication and utter security by the ardent wash of his warm kisses and the deep-throated drone of his words, blurred by entreaty and desire, I reached between our bodies and guided his cock to where it had to be.

I remembered when my mother told me she was going to die. A series of summer storms had come sweeping in from the north that day, blackening the sky. Thunder cracked and rumbled, and out of the rolling indigo clouds lightning streaked violent zigzags of eerie brilliance, its crooked rapiers plunging into the gum-clad gorges. No rain fell. In times of drought, dry storms such as this were frequent purveyors of deception. Rain almost never fell. Where the lightning found its mark, oil-impregnated eucalyptus burst instantly into flame. Coils of bluish smoke appeared here and there above the undulating hills as small fires crackled to life.

The bushfire, fanned by a hot dry wind, rapidly built in intensity until sheets of orange flame slashed the horizon, raging through the low scrub, leaping from tree to tree. Gusts of heated air bore fiery scrolls of eucalyptus bark into the sky; blazing torches that fell to the parched earth, setting new fires in brittle-dry underbrush. Sparks and glowing embers, like millions of demented fireflies, flittered everywhere. The volatile oils in the burning gums gathered in drifting gaseous clouds until they became so overheated they exploded. Tongues of fire swept along the ridgetops with a crackling roar that could be heard at the shearing shed, a mile and a half away.

Curly and all the men, even the shearing team's cook, were out fighting the fire when I returned home from school, late in the afternoon. I found my mother sitting stiffly at the kitchen table. The room was filled with lengthening blue-gray shadows and her face was strangely serene, immobile; her recently acquired pallor seemed a luminescent glow in the fading light and elongated shadows. She spoke to me so softly I could scarcely hear her words. Sobs welled up in my body and she clasped me to her and told me I was a good strong boy and I should care for and love Curly as much as she did. As the tightness left my chest and my breathing became regular, she released me from her embrace and said something I did not understand—I should not try to care for him and love him more than I would a father or he might grow to love me more than he would a son.

Brilliant light flooded the room. The first golden shafts of sunlight struck the flimsy cotton bedsheet at the window, turning each fold into a fiery tongle of flame. I clamped my lids shut against the dazzling light, against the small tremor of pain as his cock pressed into me. He entered me carefully, a little at a time to let my body become accustomed to his size. With lingering kisses on my mouth that made my whole body grow warm and open to him, he thrust his cock gently inside me. Wanting more of him, I gripped his clenched buttocks to pull him deeply into me, needing the exquisite sensation of being filled. A low buzzing pleasure coursed through all my limbs and I could feel his passion building, his frictioning thrusts becoming more urgent, more powerfully aggressive. The bedsprings bounced to his unbridled desire, crashing louder and louder as his excitement increased. I tried not to be embarrassed now, as I was when I had listened to these noises from my cot in the adjoining room.

Convolutions of light and color catherine-wheeled around the room as our bodies slapped together to some rhythmic pounding push and shove that grew only faster, faster, faster. Curly's cock was pumping in a frenzy; each inward downward plunge grunted breath out of me. An agonized curse twisted and trembled his lips and died there, half-uttered. I bit into his neck and he moaned stifled words of love, sacred and profane, into mine. Then, clinging to him with legs, arms and clawed fingers, clutching his cock with every muscle I could muster inside me, I danced my body to his tempo and brought him to a tumultuous climax. My bowels seemed to suck up and swallow his cock, out of control, convulsing, as it thickly squirted its warm juices inside me. Deep inside me, deep and potent and gut-filling.

I stroked his head, twisting small tufts of his hair between my fingers as though he were a small child. He kissed and caressed me lightly, tenderly, murmuring words I had often heard him say. His liquid kisses traveled the length of my torso, suctioning as if he might drink in my flesh, and when his lips and dipping tongue left my navel pooled with saliva, he slowly sucked my cock into his mouth. I felt myself disappear, consumed by intense velvety heat. I felt my hips spiraling, bucking uncontrollably. I heard my voice, a mewling plaintive cry. I felt myself exploding under the pressure of an immense shuddering seizure.

I smiled up into the ambient light that illuminated the ceiling, idly stretching my limbs, trying to remember how long—how many nights of feigned or half-feigned sleeping—it had taken to find myself here. Here in this room. This bed. Swirls of sunlight flashed on the ceiling, reflections of the coming day from my mother's mirror, while below a naked man and a naked boy lay more intimately entwined than ivy to ivy, lust and sweat evaporating on their bodies. Not that year, nor the next, but the year after, I would leave him. I would leave the sheep station, leave Curly's house, to make my own way in the world, because I knew, and he knew as well, that our kind of love would finally destroy us, killing the boy that I was and the kind of man I could but would not become.

"I gotta go to work, mate." His deep voice, drowsy near my ear. "An' you gotta go to school."

"Yes, boss, mister Curly," I said, tumbling across his body, kissing each of his dark nipples in turn, trailing a tongue's width of saliva across his broad chest. As he moved away from the narrow bed his massive body was briefly silhouetted against the bright tapestry of morning light. Light that brightened my smile for him. For a moment, I lay flat on my back extending all extremities, luxuriously, remember my mother had told me that I should not love him too much, that he was an orphan and his name was Cliff, but everyone called him Curly. And no one knew why.

Coming for Andy

MY MEMORY IS LIKE MY DOG. He comes when he pleases, not necessarily when I call him. But ask me about the first time I shot a load of cum into someone's mouth and my memory is right there. Snap. It's there in a flash, all excited and eager like my slobbering dog, with all the information, every little detail, crisp and clear.

My memory always begins with the misspelling on the hospital menu. They'd meant to say, I assumed, the roast lamb was going to be served with mint jelly, string beans and baked potatoes. But what it said on my breakfast tray under MENU FOR TODAY was: At five p.m. roast lamb will be *severed* with mint jelly, string beans and baked potatoes. That wasn't a word I wanted to see after running my MG off the road doing eighty, rolling it four times and depositing it, ass-up, tail-first, in a culvert. Fortunately for me, we'd parted company on the first roll.

"Stone the bloody crows, Harry," the ambulance bloke said to his offsider, scraping me out of the ditch. "He's fucking *alive.*"

I hadn't lost control on one of those vicious curves on the way up to Narrabeen (the beach where I surf, I belong to the Club), although to tell the honest truth I wish I had. That would've been less embarrassing. I'd been beetling along with the top down, singing and laughing like a loony, on a stretch of the Pacific Highway that must've been as straight as the railway tracks on the Nullarbor Plain, and you don't get any straighter than that. I mean, that's *dead* straight. Which was another word I wasn't overanxious to hear again in the near future.

"Statistically speaking, Sonny Jim, drivers in wrecks as bad as this," the police officer said, sniffing my breath, "we can pretty well count on being dead."

My memory, like my dog, isn't a hundred-per-cent trustworthy. There is an important part of the story here where it becomes evasive, skirting around some vital facts. Ask me why I left the road on a perfectly straight stretch of highway and bingo, my dog is trotting away down the road, tail up, looking for a pole or post to piss on. My memory and my dog don't have the benefits of obedience training. So my dog cocks his leg absent-mindedly and all my memory will admit to is that I demolished a bonzer little sports car for a few bruises and twenty-four stitches where I needed to be shaving. (I am up to three shaves a week.)

"There will be permanent scar tissue, of course, young fellow," this smarty-pants intern said last night, twirling his stethoscope, "but under the circumstances, you're lucky to be alive."

They wanted to watch me for a few days because I'd landed on my noggin. That was perfectly all right with me, I got to miss a few days of mental abuse at school. On the positive side I regarded the accident as a learning experience. I mean, I'd learned I'd try not to do it again. I could call it a religious experience too, on account of me rubbing noses with the Big Boss upstairs.

"But for the intervention of the Good Lord, my son," the old codger with his collar on back to front said to me this morning, "you would not have witnessed the miraculous dawning of this new day." I hadn't. I was fast asleep, as snug as a bug in a rug, having a wet dream.

The roast lamb was passable. A bit on the chewy side, and as chewing hurt I swallowed most of it in stringy lumps. The beans and spuds were mainly mush so they went down a lot easier. I ate everything except the mint jelly, which reminded me of lighter fluid. The smell more than the taste. The nurse of my dreams (wet) came in to take my pulse, blood pressure and temperature. She made me swallow a small white pill, a big yellow pill, an even bigger brown pill, and a glass of some disgusting pink stuff that made my whole body shudder as it went down. She tidied me up a bit and fussed about the bed, smoothing the sheets down, which they wouldn't because of my roaring hard-on. She was humming to herself as she left. The tune sounded familiar. I think it was "Advance Australia Fair."

"There, there, sweet pea. Don't fret." A solicitous, melodious voice. An ingratiating pat on part of my cheek not covered by bandages. "A week or so, my darling, and you'll be right as rain. With a teensy scar you'll be even more gorgeous, positively dashing." Another barrage of perfumed pats. "If we're *very* nice to Daddy, my darling, I just know he'll buy you another one of those pretty little cars." Who was this visitor? I'll give you three guesses, Right the first time. My mother, complete with a truckload of salmon pink roses. Yuk. I thought I was going to have a relapse.

My memory runs amok, I mean totally bonkers, with the mere mention of my Dad's reaction to the accident. Considering he'd bought me the MG two weeks before and I'd forgotten to mail in the insurance papers *and* I was supposed to be in school at the time, I thought his behavior was justified. Not my memory. No sir. My memory carries on like some rabid, frothing-at-the-mouth mongrel. If my memory was a dog they'd have to shoot it.

I watched the telly for a while, a game show. When this weedy drongo of a bank clerk won a sports car I got pissed off and turned it off. There's no justice in the world. None. I tried reading a comic (me being the literary type) but the pills were making me feel dopey. I couldn't stay focused. I flipped the switch to the overhead light, leaving the bedside table lamp on. I can't sleep in the dark. It's not that I'm afraid or anything, it's just that I've always slept with a light on. I suppose you'd call it a habit.

My memory excels itself in retrieving the events that followed. My damp-nosed dog, on rare occasions, gets wildly excited and races up to me at full speed, legs like windmills, and dumps a mouthful of something—rags, bones, chicken shit, anything—at my feet. That's how my memory delivers the gory details of what happened next.

I didn't have a clue what time it was or how long I'd been sleeping when he came into the room. I woke up. Zap. And there he was, a figure dressed in white placing an instrument tray on the bedside table. In hospital that's not unusual. The thing that struck me as unusual, though, wasn't that it was a bloke, but that the door to my room was closed. I'd never seen the door to my room closed since I'd been there. I mean, its always being open seemed like some kind of *rule*.

Moving to the end of my bed, he picked up my chart and was scanning it. He looked up and said, "I am the night nurse. My name is Andrew Bainbridge." He smiled in a businesslike way and sat down on the edge of my bed. "But you may call me Andy." His smile, with these words, switched to friendly. Reassuring. Almost intimate. He had a pleasant, open face, brightly handsome, the sort of face that reminds you of someone you know well. His eyes were clear blue and sparkling. I thought he looked more like one of my surfer mates than a nurse, but as I'd only seen female nurses, what did I know.

Andy relaxed his position on my bed, slumping a little, letting his arm rest against my thigh. The way a good friend might. His arm was warm and comfortable. "Perhaps you are wondering why we are making this visit so late in the evening," he said. I wasn't, I was eyeing the room around, looking for the other half of the plural pronoun. "Your doctor has requested some special tests. Due to the nature of these tests he thought it preferable they be conducted by a male nurse during the convenience and privacy of an evening hour. Nothing to be concerned about. These matters, simply, are better dealt with man to man." He flashed his reassuring smile. I smiled back. Reassured. I liked the idea of being dealt with man to man. I felt grown up. Mature.

"Apart from the sutured laceration and minor, superficial abrasions, your state of health, physically, emotionally, psychologically, is excellent," Andy was saying, patting my thigh, then standing. "However, your doctor requires that proof be evidenced of the unimpaired functionality of the reproductive organs. Unless you have questions, we will commence the tests without further ado." I shook my head, meaning no questions. Actually, I had several, but I didn't want to sound like an idiot.

"To facilitate the procedure," he said, taking off his white jacket and rolling up his shirt sleeves, "all encumbrances should be removed." He stripped back the top sheet with a flourish that would've made a toreador proud. "Unfasten these, please." He made a little jab at the top button of my pajama shirt. "I will attend to the lower garment." I felt fingers undoing the cord at my waist and hands pulling down my pajama pants. I was glad the bandages concealed a lot of my face. I was blushing like a schoolgirl. The rush of cool air did feel nice on my cock, though.

Andy helped me out of my shirt. (Don't laugh. Try it sometime. Lie on your back and take off your shirt.) "You have an excellent physique, my friend," he said, looking down at me stretched out naked on the bed. "The development of the musculature is quite impressive. You do a lot of swimming?" I nodded. (If you haven't noticed, words and sports cars have something in common for me—I can't seem to handle them.) "Ah yes, I thought as much," he said, moving in closer, placing his hands lightly on my chest. A warm palm covered each nipple. "A young Adonis... astoundingly beautiful..." I wasn't sure that's what he'd said. His voice was so low, inwardly directed, as if he'd slipped into some private world.

Andy quickly removed his hands, and stepping back, regained his businesslike voice. "If you are able to relax completely, not be nervous or embarrassed, the tests will be more accurate." Reaching forward, he touched the tips of his fingers to my stomach. "Hmm, splendid abdominals. Six perfectly formed cobblestones." He laughed and did a two-finger, bouncy walk across my belly. I tightened up, bunching the muscles (I'm particularly proud of these muscles, my body in general) which made his stiff-legged fingers bounce all the more. That tickled, so now we were both laughing. I was pleased he liked my build, flattered by his praise. It was easy to be relaxed with him.

"Fortunately, we are able to dispense with the urine sample.

Adequate specimens have already been taken." I nodded. I'd hated pissing into the bottle with the nurse hovering impatiently behind me. With Andy, though, I wouldn't have minded at all.

Andy was pressing his palms against my stomach, kneading and squeezing, working deeply under the muscles with his fingers. "Any pain there?" he asked. I shook my head. His hands were strong, his fingeers supple and experienced. It was a good feeling. Slowly, his hands traveled up to my chest, massaging in small circular movements. I closed my eyes, enjoying his touch, enjoying each series of sensations as he worked my muscles. Lulled by warm waves of pure pleasure, I let myself drift into a sort of drowsy half-sleep.

"Mmm... marvelous pectorals, absolutely marvelous," he was saying. I didn't bother to nod. I knew I had great pecs, and besides, he seemed to be talking to himself again. Saying aloud the things he was thinking.

Suddenly, whew! Little electric shocks were zapping all the way down to my toes. I opened my eyes to see why. Andy was pinching my nipples, pinching and twisting them. It hurt, but yet it didn't, if that makes any sense. "Erectile tissue is responding appropriately," he said, with his outside voice. My nipples looked like two miniature Mount Everests. Only red instead of white. His fingers flicked each peak, which sent a funny feeling straight to my groin. Really weird. I mean, him doing things to my tits was giving me a nice, quivery feeling between my legs.

"Now, we must inspect the testes," he said, "or testicles as you probably know them." I knew them as balls. Or nuts. "Maneuver yourself towards me and open your legs wide, please." I did. I felt very exposed. Not just naked, I mean very *exposed.*

Andy sat on the triangle of bed between my veed legs and put his hands on my thighs, squeezing gently. "Mmmm, amazing. Amazing muscle tone," he said to himself, stroking and squeezing my legs. Then to me, he said, "The testes, my friend are much-maligned organs. Seemingly insignificant, inconspicuously situated, comprising less than one thousandth part of the human male's body weight, they are, both in his mind and in reality, the root of a man's potency." I wasn't going to argue with that. So I nodded. His hands were still on my thighs, stroking, inching closer to my balls, which were beginning to bunch up, tight and tingling. He was still talking.

"The testes not only manufacture sperm for the creation of new life, but they produce hormones repsonsible for the development and function of a young man's penis, for the deepening of his voice, the growth of his body hair, the burgeoning of his muscles, increasing dramatically their bulk and power. They are..." His hands moved in and cupped my balls, cradling them in his joined palms like... "precious jewels."

"Priceless and exquisite," he was muttering as he patted my balls and jiggled them in different directions and bounced them up and down. I didn't mind it at all. It felt strange, but nice. Separating them with careful fingers, holding each one individually, he felt all around them. His touch was so light his fingers seemed like feathers. Then he pressed them together, tightly together, applying pressure. A ripple of dull pain made me grunt. "Aha! Sensitive, eh!" He had a gleam in his eye. "Good! Good! Obviously no numbing there." He gave another good squeeze, to be sure I suppose. I gave another grunt.

Andy relaxed the pressure on my balls but continued to fondle them with one hand while the other lightly caressed my inner thighs. "Does that cause a pleasant, tickling sensation?" he asked. I nodded. The sensation was so much more than pleasantly tickling. And it was making my cock sit up and take notice. It twitched a few times then started looking around, its head snaking out across my belly. "What do we have here?" Andy asked, noticing. "Do I detect an engorgement of the flaccid penis?" He was rubbing his hands together. "An erection, without doubt, is in progress." He looked like he'd just found a fortune in buried treasure. "Excellent! Exactly what we had hoped for, a perfectly normal response to specific, zonal stimulation."

Both Andy and I were looking at my cock, watching it

grow bigger and thicker by the second. "Why do Eskimos need refrigerators?" he asked, smiling broadly. I shook my head. I didn't know what he was talking about. I was trying to concentrate on keeping my cock from getting hard. "You do not know why Eskimos need refrigerators?" I shook my head. I was losing the battle with my cock. He laughed. "How else could they keep their food from freezing? Ha! Ha!" I would have laughed too, but I had too much to think about. I had a big problem. My cock. It was hard, heavy and hard, like a piece of lead pipe. And Andy was holding it in his hand.

"Ah, yes. Magnificent," he was saying, moving his hand slowly up and down. "Even more magnificent than we had imagined." I'd never had another person's hand on my cock before. I had to admit it was a pretty wonderful feeling. "The columns of porous tissue are engorged to their maximum. The rigidity is outstanding." He kept squeezing the shaft of my cock in his fist as he spoke, and I liked what he was doing so much that I decided having a hard-on was no longer a problem. I mean, if he wasn't embarrassed, why should I be.

"While we have the penis fully distended we will take advantage of this condition for the next series of tests," he said, reaching to the instrument tray with his free hand. "But first, a measurement." He held a tape measure up against the side of my cock. "Ah, how impressive. How *very* impressive. Eight and five-eighths inches, and still a growing lad."

Secretly, I was pleased my cock had made an impression on Andy. His excitement somehow excited me. I knew I was big. My surfer mates and I saw each other naked in the showers all the time, and my cock was by far the biggest. They ogled my crotch with envy, watching my cock flop about, watching it get even bigger as I soaped it up. And I'd do that on purpose. I'd get it growing, not real hard mind you, but hard enough to see their jealous looks. Let's face it, I like to show off my body, I like to be looked at. I mean, that's natural. As my dippy mother says, "If you've got it, my darling, don't hide it. Flaunt it." I guess I'm a bit of an exhibitionist at heart.

Andy was sliding his warm fist up and down the entire length of my cock. I wriggled my hips to let him know he was getting me hot and bothered. He explained, "It is necessary that we provide a little manual stimulation to maintain the erect state of the organ." A *little* stimulation, he said. I can tell you things were getting pretty severe down there. His hand was moving fast and the stimulation was intense. I mean, very intense. If he didn't stop soon, I was going to shoot off in his hand. I heard myself groan, and Andy didn't stop, he pumped faster. My body was writhing, my hips bucked up off the bed, I gripped the sheets and groaned again. "Yes! Yes! Yes!" he was saying and I was shooting my load. My cum spurted up across my body; the first big rush whizzed past my ear, splatting the wall behind the bed. Splat. Splat. Splat. The rest went all over my chest and belly.

"A remarkable ejaculation," Andy said, with his professional smile, as I sucked in oxygen. "The distance of projection far exceeded the norm, as did the quantity of seminal fluid discharged." He squeezed the head of my cock between finger and thumb and more cum came flowing out. "Do you produce an equally copious amount of ejaculate with your own self-induced orgasms?" What he meant was, I think, did I cum this much when I jerked off. I nodded, wondering if I was abnormal. "Quite remarkable," he said, attending diligently to my cock for its last few trickles. "A truly outstanding performance." I assumed I wasn't abnormal, merely well-above-average. I liked that.

I watched Andy playing with the cum on my chest. He was spreading it around, slathering my skin, dabbling in it with his fingers. "The color is good. Density, opacity and viscosity, all excellent." He picked up a small stainless-steel bowl and, with a spatula, scooped up the globs of cum from my chest and belly. "Laboratory samples are required for the sperm count and other tests," he said as he returned the bowl to the tray. He licked around his fingers, meticulously, the way a kid does when his ice cream cone dribbles. (That's what my memory says he did, but I don't believe it.) Unfolding a soft, damp towel, he wiped the front of my body, spending a lot of time patting and dabbing at my cock. Then he asked me to roll over onto my stomach.

Andy slipped a pillow under my hips which made my bum stick up in the air. He said he needed to take my temperature. A pretty peculiar position to get your temperature taken, I thought. I twisted my neck to see what he was up to. He was squeezing some stuff, a sort of colorless jelly, onto his finger, and he had a thermometer in his mouth.

"Please spread your legs to a comfortable width, my friend," he said. "Be assured that this will cause you no discomfort." His voice was half-strangled, because of the thermometer held between his teeth. He looked and sounded funny. I laughed. Taking out the thermometer he flicked it three times. "Ha! Ha!" he laughed, too. "We warm the thermometer orally for a few seconds, otherwise the chill can be a shock to sensitive nerve endings and delicate membranes." He was patting my buttocks as he explained, much the same way I pat my dog when he retrieves the old boot I've thrown. I was beginning to have a strong suspicion as to where he was going to put the thermometer.

Andy parted my bum cheeks and squeezed out more clear stuff from the tube. A big dollop landed right on my asshole. Yeow! It was cold. My hips jerked into the pillow. He wasn't wrong about the sensitive nerve endings.

"Please be still," he said, poking at my asshole with the jellied tip of his finger. "We are about to make the insertion." I held my breath, bracing myself, ready for the worst. The thermometer slid in easily and it wasn't cold. I was thankful he'd warmed it in his mouth, and breathed a sigh of relief. It was a strange feeling having the thermometer inside me. I mean, sort of interesting, and certainly not unpleasant.

"Relax, let all the muscles relax," Andy was saying in a low, crooning voice. "Yes, like that. Good, very good. Try not to contract the sphincter." If I'd known what it was I wouldn't have. He was jiggling the thermometer around inside me, then pulling it out and sliding it back in. The jiggling felt nice. The pulling and pushing was even nicer. I liked having my temperature taken this way. I was sorry when Andy finally took it out.

"Good, he's put the thermometer back in my ass." That's

what I thought at first, when the nice feeling was back there again. But it wasn't stiff like the thermometer, it was bending in different directions, feeling warmer, going deeper. And it was so much bigger. "It's not the thermometer," I realized. "It's his finger. He's got his damn finger up my asshole."

"There are glands we must check, deep inside," Andy said, pushing his finger deeper still. "Please remain as relaxed as possible." But my bum was squirming like crazy as his finger poked about, way up inside my asshole. His finger, wriggling like a hungry snake, felt a thousand times better than the thermometer. It was impossible to stay relaxed.

"The prostate evidences no swelling." Andy sounded pleased with this discovery, but whatever it was that wasn't swelling, it wasn't my cock. If I was getting a charge from having his finger up my ass, my cock was getting a supercharge. It was rock hard, throbbing and stabbing into the pillow.

Andy's finger was moving in and out of my asshole at the exact same speed as my cock trying to fuck the pillow. He seemed to be doing it deliberately, as if his finger was fucking my ass. My whole body was thrashing around on the bed and I was groaning again. I couldn't help it. Things were building fast. Andy's finger was a red-hot poker, going like lightning. I couldn't hold back any longer, I was ready to let fly another load. At that very moment, he flipped me over onto my back and in that one split second I saw my cock jerk up, his head poised over it. I watched the first jet of cum squirt into his open mouth. Then my cock disappeared. All eight and five-eighths inches of it. Gone. He'd swallowed it whole. I was coming and coming. I couldn't believe it, I mean the stuff had to be going somewhere. But where? Into his mouth, down his throat? Where?

Andy sat back and smiled. It wasn't his professional smile; he looked like a little boy caught being naughty. "Sorry about that, my friend." His tongue flicked out over his lips. "We had no warning on the taste test. There was insufficient time to explain the procedure." His naughty grin broadened. "Do you usually achieve a climax with such expedition?" I shook my head. I mean, I cum fast, but not *that* fast. Of course, I don't usually have someone fingering my asshole either. That made a big difference, I can tell you.

"You will be pleased to know the semen quality is first-rate." Andy was back in his professional mode. "A subtle underlying hint of freshly sliced cucumber is a noteworthy indication of a healthy ejaculate." As he spoke I noticed a blob of white swirling on his pink tongue. My cum. He licked his lips, swallowed, and said, "Semen is rich in protein and vitamin C, as well as containing fructose and a number of enzymes, bicarbonates and phosphates, and happily, almost no calories."

Moving to the bedside table, Andy checked over the list on his clipboard, making neat little ticks with a ballpoint pen. "Well, my friend, we have accomplished enough for tonight. We do not want to overtax the patient, do we?" I shook my head, although I didn't feel in the least bit overtaxed. As he began tidying up, rearranging his tray, he said, "Tomorrow night, we will check the major erogenous zones for sensitivity response and arousal rate, we will take additional semen samples, conducting further taste tests to be assured quality is being maintained, and we will need to employ the services of the rectal probe." From his tray he held up a pinkish-colored rubber thing with torpedo-shaped ends. It was easiliy twelve inches long and almost as thick around as my wrist. I couldn't imagine what he was planning to do with that.

Andy helped me back into my pajamas, tucked the sheet in carefully and fluffed my pillow. "Thank you, my friend," he said, sitting on the edge of my bed. "You are the most co-operative patient we have ever had." He tousled my hair. "And certainly the most handsome." He placed his hand on the sheet, on the bulge of my crotch, and gave it a little squeeze. "Now promise me, no masturbating prior to tomorrow night. We need all the semen you can manufacture for the tests." I nodded. My cock nodded, too. He gave it another squeeze. Both my cock and I were looking forward to tomorrow night.

"G'night, Andy," I called out to the white-coated figure

disappearing down the dark corridor. I noticed he hadn't closed the door as he left my room.

It was still dark when this old drab of a nurse woke me up. She shook out a thermometer and stuck it under my tongue. I watched her lining up the pills. There was no pink liquid, thank the Good Lord, who had intervened once again on my behalf. Her prissy, goody-goody manner irritated me. When she flipped the thermometer out of my mouth I told her the night nurse had already taken my temperature, and just to aggravate the old sow, I announced, "And he put it up my ass." She shot me a glance that nailed me to the mattress, her mouth going square and ugly. "*I* am the night nurse." Her voice rattled the room, my teeth included. "There are no *male* nurses on the staff of this hospital, nor are rectal thermometers in use here." She huffed her starched-white barrel body through the door, muttering something about keeping my "lurid, adolescent dreams" to myself.

My memory plays the same game my dog plays. My dog loves to fetch this scruffy, old leather boot. I throw it and he chases after it until it stops rolling. Before he pounces, he crouches low, not moving a muscle, barely breathing, pretending he isn't there. For a moment, after the nurse left the room, I thought my memory was playing the game. I looked through the iron bedframe behind me. The splodges of cum were there on the wall, not even dried up yet. Living proof. I whipped back the sheet and undid my pajama bottoms, and smiled. My memory wasn't playing stupid pet tricks; I hadn't dreamed up Andy. My cock was napping on my thigh, fat and happy, a dribble of cum at its head. There was no sign in the bed of the second load I'd shot. All that cum had to be somewhere. My cock and I knew where.

Ask me what happened the next night and I've nothing to report. Zip. When Andy came into my room with his tray and closed the door behind him, my memory stayed outside in the corridor. I told you. My memory is like my dog. He comes to me when he pleases.

Aussie Hot

LOOKING BACK OVER MY LIFE, trying to make some sense of the nonsense of it all, I have come to believe that the manifestation of one's adult sexuality is just a plexus, a cocoon constructed around a few early experiences.

One such youthful encounter that lies safely enshrined at the core of my life's densely woven mantle led to my seduction, at age fifteen, by a mysterious stranger—a man twice my own age—an itinerant farm laborer self-exiled from another country to my small world in the outback of Australia.

I remember well the day I first met the stranger. Like any other January day in Queensland's sheep country it was too hot to be outdoors. Altogether too hot and too bright. And like all the other days of my school holidays, boredom and despair finally drove me from the cool confines of the veranda, having spent interminable hours of entombment there, reading and daydreaming since early morning. That day, as any other day, I crossed the well-watered, manicured lawns and walked through the lattice-covered arbor where the bougainvillea that hung about it—tumbling festoons of livid magenta—glared stridently in the sunlight.

No life stirred in the arid, afternoon heat. Finches and wrens drooped like dead leaves in the shrubbery and my dog lay stretched out and limp on the damp earth under a garden tap, paws and ears and tail all reaching out, flattened, to absorb the coolness. As I passed by he rolled his eyes at me, two white marbles in blood-red sockets, and his tail twitched but did not lift from the comfortable dirt.

Minutes later, when I climbed the split-rail fence that enclosed the home paddock, a score or more of white cockatoos suddenly fell out of the eucalyptus trees like a riot of swirling handkerchieves, shrieking annoyance at my presence. Then, sorting themselves noisily into loose formation, they streaked away, evaporating into the shimmering sky. That day, like all the days before it, I walked to the creek to swim.

* * *

THE STRANGER CAME to the homestead at dusk when bats darted in tattered silhouette against the darkening indigo sky. He stood in front of the open shed and talked to my dad until all that could be seen of the two men was the spiraling dot of red light from the stranger's cigarette. His slow, twangy drawl carried through the heat-heavy evening air to the veranda where I sat sprawling in a wicker rocking chair. I strained to hear, fascinated by the deep, undulating resonance of the man's voice. There was something about it, an intonation, a timbre, which was like nothing I had ever heard before. Something that caused the skin on my nape and the backs of my bare thighs to tingle warmly.

"He's looking for work," my dad told Mum later, arguing about the stranger in the kitchen.

"I don't like the looks of him," Mum kept repeating. "He's different from the rest. Strange-looking and... well, just different."

"He *is* different," Dad agreed. He had an alibi for the difference. "He's American—"

"I don't give a bugger what he is, I don't like the looks of him."

"—and an ex-marine."

"Looks more like an ex-convict to me."

"We need him. And I've hired him." Dad's voice trailed in the wake of hers, truculent, but resolute.

"That's your funeral. But don't come back later telling me..." I retuned my ears to other, less strident, night sounds and thought about the stranger. The American. The new worker taken on by my dad to help with the shearing who I had met that same afternoon while swimming in a secluded creek a mile and a half from the homestead. Swimming naked as I swam there every afternoon in the summer holidays. The creek was on our property, miles from the main road in a heavily timbered valley, reachable only on foot from the house. Nobody ever went there, except me. Until that day.

I was not swimming when he came, but sleeping. A clump of scrubbly banksias overhanging the creek bed gave me shade enough to doze pleasantly, though fitfully, in the gravelly red sand. My eyes were opened from a vanishing dream to an emerging reality by a disquieting sensation, an eerie, almost shocking awareness of being observed. I sat up abruptly, rubbing my eyes to regain sight, waiting for the surroundings to come into focus. I heard the voice before I saw the speaker.

"Hi there, sleepyhead."

The sing-sing of melodious words made my skin prickle with an uneasy flush of embarrassment, making me acutely aware of my nakedness, even more acutely aware of my cock standing erect and rampant. Squinting into the light I could see the outline of the intruder's body; the squatting shape of a man close by, featureless with the sun behind him. Though not able to distinguish the details of his face, his eyes, I felt their scrutiny on my body, appraising me the way a judge might closely inspect a prize bull calf at a cattle show. A critical appreciation of a young male animal in its prime.

"Who the hell are you? What're you doing here?" My voice caught in my throat, dry and raspy, scarcely audible. Defensive.

"Hi! I'm just a bum," the intruder laughed, and moved closer. "Just a Yankee bum, passing through."

"A . . . a bum?" I stammered, not comprehending, realizing the accent was unusual, not ours, not Australian.

"Yeah, a bum." He laughed again, moving still closer. "But a harmless one." The sun now lit him from the side and I saw what manner of man this stranger was. He was thick-limbed, stocky, bull-necked, with bulging biceps heavily tattooed and a face that was square and full-fleshed, appearing both innocently boyish and roguishly old at the same time. The rough, rust-brown stubble on his jaw continued up his cheeks and higher, wrapping his skull. It was the first crewcut I had ever seen. Hair on his eyebrows was bleached by the sun, but they were mostly brown, the same reddish-brown as the growth on his face and the brush bristles that covered his head. He had a puckish, snub nose and his lips were dark and full, curling up at the corners in a contemptuous half-smile that showed a top tooth missing in the side of his mouth. He was not handsome, yet he was not ugly either. The aura about him was magnetic and compelling, not wholly angelic nor entirely barbaric, but suffused equally with elements of both.

"You shouldn't be here," I said, trying to find authority in my voice. "This is private property."

"Sure. Anything you say, fella." His manner was too friendly, too intimate. I shivered in the dry-dust heat of the afternoon and my blood quickened with a strange excitement that coursed through my body and kept my cock painfully erect.

"If my dad knew you were here he'd..."

"But he don't know does he? Unless someone's gonna tell him. And who's gonna do a dumbshit thing like that? Who now?" He enunciated each question slowly and deliberately, not threatening but mocking me, taunting me, sweetly challenging me with conniving, liquid smiles. "Would it be you, fella? Would you tell him? Would you, huh?"

In sudden panic I lurched forward to rise to my feet, but his hand shot out and gripped my shoulder. The grip was strong, powerful, not enough to cause pain but enough to keep me sitting half-stunned and immobile in the sand. I felt an icy blade of fear slice through me from the back of my neck to the pit of my stomach. It was the first time in all my fifteen years that I had experienced real, gut-cleaving fear. But fear of what exactly, I did not know. I did not believe that this enigmatic stranger, all smiles and charming guile, intended to do me bodily harm. Still, somehow, the maleness he exuded seemed potently aggressive and his physical proximity unnerved me. Despite my confusion and almost palpable dread, my cock stood throbbing with a renewed, inexplicable hardness.

"You ain't gonna tell, falla, are you?" His face was inches from mine, his voice purring. It could have been a plea.

"No," I whispered, holding my breath at some inner, unexpected flickering as his hand squeezed the bare flesh of my shoulder. "No, I'm not going to tell." And I breathed.

"Atta boy. I knew we was gonna be good buddies." His hand moved from my shoulder and passed in a blur in front of my eyes to tousle my hair, roughly at first, then playfully, almost gently, the way Dad used to before I grew to be as tall and broad-shouldered as he.

"Real good buddies, you and me," he said, his voice near my ear, crooning, persuasive. I felt the warm exhalation of words on my cheek and another warmth, uncoiling inside me. A big work-rough hand glided lightly down the side of my face, down the curve of my neck, loosening a damp twist of curls, lingering in the indented hollow at the base of my throat, lingering then moving down again, to my chest to deftly massage the swell of muscle there. I shivered. No one had ever touched my body like that before.

"Mmm . . . real good," he murmured, and surprisingly delicate, trailing fingertips gave me precise little shocks of excitement wherever they touched and his voice seemed to confirm whatever his hands were saying. Insinuating and cajoling. Enticing. "Good buddies who know how to take care of each other. Real good care."

I tried to dissemble the tremor of challenge and temptation the stranger's words aroused in me. I understood vaguely what he meant; the implications of his words in my ear, his hands on my body becoming clearer as I listened to a language which had been foreign to me until then. I knew those things—the things he was saying and doing—were suggestive, were fraught with overt entreaty and illicit sexual possibilities, but I did not know how or in what manner they could be accomplished. I was certain, however, something was about to happen that was right and wrong and natural, and knowing this I was both terrified and delirious with anticipation.

"You're one helluva hot young stud," he growled in my ear, biting the lobe, thrusting inside with a slithery, snake-like tongue. Probing deeply.

"Don't . . ." I gasped. "Please, don't . . ." And gasped again as fingers and thumbs pinched and twisted my nipples. "Oh, please . . . don't." His hands were everywhere, touching, squeezing, caressing every part of my body, the pleasure at once both vaporous and explicit. And totally irresistible. Small involuntary cries kept escaping from my lips.

"Please stop . . . Oh, please stop . . ." But I was hopelessly lost to the incredible, hungry carnality that rose thickly in me. And mercifully, he did not stop.

"Oh, please . . . Oh, please . . ." I choked, desperately needing him not to stop, not wanting him to stop, not *ever* wanting him to stop.

"Please . . . Oh . . . Please . . ." I cried out, and his hands were there, between my legs. My balls were gripped. My cock's turgid shaft was gripped. Everything gripped in clutching, consuming fists, the pleasure all-pervading and complete.

"Oh . . . Oh . . ." And my knees gave way and muscle and sinew and bone turned to jelly, and I collapsed into his body, into his embrace, my cock thrusting again and again into the soft-worn denim of his thigh, thrusting and exploding, squirting pulsing jets of cum against his leg. Thrusting and squirting.

For a few quandaried moments of disoriented aftermath he held me securely in his arms, cradling me close to his body like a helpless child. Then gradually, the awful reality, the abject horror of what had happened penetrated my numbed brain. I began to tremble uncontrollably and tears of guilt and humiliation flowed silently down my cheeks. Struggling violently, I wrenched myself away from him with such force he fell backward into the sand.

"You're a real firecracker, aintcha?" He was laughing, amused by my plight, laughing at my consternation. He ran his hand down the leg of his jeans where large patches showed darkly wet with my soaked-up discharge. "Jesus, fella, that big dong of yours shoots like a goddamn cannon."

Feeling nothing but shame and confusion, I clambered awkwardly into my shorts and tee-shirt. The man's coarseness and hilarity was little more than background noise to the clamor of suffocating remorse that had descended on me.

"I'm sorry . . . I'm really sorry . . ." I stammered, my eyes in the sand at his boots, not daring to look at his face, not knowing why I was apologizing. It was all I could think to say before I turned and ran, heading for the scrubby underbrush. Heading for home.

* * *

AND NOW HE WAS HERE. The stranger was here—a newly recruited laborer on our sheep station—sleeping not a hundred yards from my bedroom where I lay in agonized and sweating recollection of the afternoon at the creek, sleeping in the loft space of the fodder storage shed, not because the shearers' quarters were full but because he was not one of them. Not one of their team. Different.

And here I was, struggling with the consequences of his artful manipulation, trying to justify, trying to excuse myself of any wrongdoing, for surely what he had done to me was wrong, loathesome, a sin against nature in God's all-seeing eyes. Otherwise why should I have suffered such torment of self-reproach and shame. But what had he actually *done?* He had spoken to me, placed his hands on my body, aroused me, while I—half-fearing, half-wanting—made myself available to his advances without contest. Had I given myself up to temptation or merely a fantasy of temptation; my fantasy of robust and virile men who stirred some elusive longing inside me? While his hands caressed my naked body there had been no disgust, no guilt, just pure, soaring pleasure. Degradation and self-disgust came later. But why? Why?

In the shuttered security of my room, my loathing for the stranger, for myself, was softened by a gentle wave of more complex and subtle emotions, diminished by a nascent lust licking like a flame through my outstretched limbs. Reaching down, I touched and tentatively held what I perceived to be the essence of my discontent. My cock, already thickened by prurient thoughts of recent pleasure, quivered in readiness for further erotic adventure. I stroked its broad shaft, comforted by the pleasurable sensations welling within me, the rekindling of a seemingly insatiable need. Reassured by my cock's anxious demand, the vigorous response of its meaty thickness, its assertiveness, I felt the undulating ebb of all previous fear. That singular, insistent voice was a voice without guilt or shame that I would listen to now above all else.

Mum had said: "I don't like the looks of him."

My dad said: "He *is* different."

My heart was saying: "He is the one."

He had told me: "You're one helluva hot young stud."

My cock, agreeing with all of them and none of them, said: "Go for it."

Without lighting the lamp, feeling around on the floor at the foot of my bed, I located the clothes I had worn that afternoon. The tee-shirt stank and the front of my shorts, I knew, displayed an obvious stain where my cock had leaked, sprinting away from the creek. Body odor and blemishes were of no importance to me. Being physically admired and sexually sought after filled me with a self-confidence, an enormously inflated self-image, that mere clothes could not further enhance. For action not effect, I dressed hurriedly.

In the murky, fetid depths of the storage shed, mounting the ladder to the loft less and less purposefully, my recently acquired confidence sank as I rose. On reaching the topmost rung, I faltered. My cock—a dangling, shriveled prune—had lost its voice, and for the second time that day I felt the swordthrust of fear in my bowels. I moved to descend.

"Who's there?"

I sucked in air and froze. I heard the sounds of a lantern being lit. Orange light flickered then glowed on the criss-cross network of beams overhead. Shadows formed and advanced as amorphous patches of darkness receded.

"Who the fuck is it?"

I exhaled slowly and poked my head above the platform of wooden planks, and said, feebly, "It's me.""

At first all I could see was the glaring brightness of the kerosene lantern, but as my eyes grew accustomed to the light, I saw him propped up against a support post at the far end of the loft space. He was barechested and barefoot, possibly completely naked under the threadbare gray blanket that covered him from hips to ankles. I noticed a duffle bag and other belongings strewn about on the wide-board flooring. There was a bottle beside the post and another in his right hand; the pungent, dry-rot smell of cheap whiskey that lingered in the air was not incompatible with the shed's own dank odor of fertilizer and musty hay. The smile on his face was familiar, the full-lipped, slightly contemptuous, rogue's smile.

"You're late," he drawled, widening his grin.

"Late . . . ?" I saw in his face, in his laughing eyes, that he was enjoying my bewilderment.

"Yeah. Thought you'd be here an hour ago."

"But . . . But, how . . . How did you know I lived here?"

"Shit, where else, fella," he guffawed, waving the bottle in an erratic arc over his head. "There ain't another outfit like this in fifty miles."

"But I didn't . . ."

"Quit yakking, why dontcha, and climb aboard." He lit a cigarette, pluming blue smoke into the rafters, and carelessly flicked the match into the depths below.

"You shouldn't do that." Too late, I bit my tongue.

"Still telling me what I should and shouldn't do, eh sonny boy?" His voice was hard-edged, no laughter left in it.

"I'm sorry . . ."

"And still saying you're sorry for everything. What sorta man are you, anyway?"

"I'm . . . " This time I bit my tongue in time, and thinking fast said, "Dad said you were a marine."

His spine pulled up straight and he snapped a professional salute, spilling whiskey down the front of his chest. "Lance Corporal Everett Harvey Bonner, United States Marine Corps, reporting to duty, *sir!*" I watched the amber liquid trace a serpentine course through the creases of his stomach and pool into his navel, feeling relieved to hear him laugh easily again. "Make yourself at home," he said, thumping the floorboards with the flat of his hand. He held out the bottle to me, making a priest's gesture of blessing with it. "Have a drink, fella. It'll put hair on your chest."

"I can't," I said, sitting cross-legged by his left side. "I'm not old enough."

"Bullshit. You're old enough to have hair on your dick. I seen it meself this afternoon."

"I mean, drink . . . I'm not supposed to."

"You're not supposed to do a lotta things." He gave me a knowing wink that screwed up one side of his face and reached out his free hand to squeeze my thigh. "But you do 'em anyway, dontcha?" My cock responded immediately to his touch, his innuendo, swelling rapidly and visibly outlining itself in my shorts. Hoping to distract its progress, no longer able to deal with its newfound voice, I snatched the bottle away from the man and tilted it to my lips. Bitter fumes filled my nose and mouth. I managed to stifle a cough but could not stop my eyes from watering. I rubbed them with my forearm, still clutching the bottle. My throat burned and I swallowed to fight back an uprushing of rejected whiskey and bile. And to all of that my cock was oblivious, intent on its own purpose.

I could feel the hand on my thigh inching along my leg toward the crotch of my shorts, the bulge there growing bigger as it drew nearer. *Keep calm,* I told myself, panic rising, *this is why you came, this is what you want.* I pretended not to notice the hand, telling myself the dread I felt was irrational, childish. Warm fingers slid under the leg of my shorts. My balls seemed touched with delicate flutterings. Time stopped, or sped. Delving fingers found my cock—*this is what you want*—traveled its rigid length, manipulating—*what you want him to do*—encircling—*want him to do to you*—squeezing. I gasped, and not wanting to say it, I said, "No! No, don't." The words were strangled in the stricture of my throat and came out as nothing more than a breathy groan. But he sensed my distress.

Taking the bottle from my hand he placed it carefully on the floor behind the post and touched my cheek, applying pressure so that I would look at his face. I was trembling. His eyes were black in the dimness, black and intense. He looked at me for a while, not saying anything; just looking at me with shining eyes filled with warmth and caring and want. Then he said, "You're a good-looking kid," and smiled, "a real knock-out." I blushed, blinked a few times but made my eyes stay with his. And they held mine, unblinking, with that wet brightness, that intensity, of alcohol and sexual need, and his hand still down there on my cock was not squeezing anymore, but cradling.

"I won't do nothing if you don't wanna," he said.

I nodded my head, down and up. I did not know whether that meant yes or no, so I said, "It's okay." I was not sure, but my trembling had stopped.

The hand on my cheek dropped away and I let my eyes follow. He placed it on my crotch, shaping it around the tubular outline of my cock so that I was held now with two hands, one inside the fabric and one outside.

"A great-looking kid," he said, "with a beautiful cock."

I watched the muscles on his forearm change shape as his hands became articulate between my legs, and concealed an unexpected smile, for it had never occurred to me to think of my cock as beautiful. Sunrise skies, some of Mum's dresses, the sweeping brilliance of butterfly wings were beautiful.

"You're sure it's okay?" he asked. And not merely asking in a polite way, but with a heart-felt sincerity that deepened his voice.

I nodded. "Yeah. It's okay."

And it was this time, it really was.

I did not move a muscle as his hands roamed all over my body, as if he was searching for yet-undiscovered parts of me to explore. I sat like a department store dummy because I did not know what else to do. I kept telling my body to relax, do something with itself, but I did not want to distract him or appear to lack the proper seriousness. He pulled my tee-shirt out of my shorts and rucked it up across my chest, exposing my midriff. Dipping his head, he pressed his lips to my bare flesh, licking me there, moving all over my belly, licking and kissing the skin. His tongue circled my navel then jabbed it over and over, swabbing it with saliva. Holding my shirt up to my chin, he lapped a wet trail to my chest, kissing and nibbling and sucking on each nipple.

I let my arms go limp so that he could pull the tee-shirt over my head more easily, thinking that I probably looked like a rabbit being skinned. While he undid the button at the waistband of my shorts and while his fingers, descending, pushed each successive button through its hole, he made little closed-mouth humming sounds. Straightening my legs—grateful for something helpful to do, to participate—I pushed weight into my heels to raise my buttocks, and he pulled my unfastened shorts away from my hips, down my thighs, over my knees to my ankles, in a long sweeping flourish. My released cock sprang up against my belly with an audible slap.

"Lie back, fella. All the way," he said, his voice as gentle as my mum's, when she used to tuck me in at night.

I lowered my buttocks and curled my back to the floorboards, feeling each vertebra connect. With my arms extended over my head, right thumb caught in left fist, I realized I was once again naked in the eyes of the stranger, as naked and vulnerable as before, but now rid of all feelings of abuse and embarrassment and shame. And without a scrap, one iota, of guilt.

The gray blanket fell away as he knelt over me, and glimpses of his crouching body confirmed his own nakedness. When I felt my cock enclosed in warmth and wetness I closed my eyes and my breath came out in a long, sustained sigh. That he would take my cock into his mouth was something I believed could happen, but I was not prepared for—would not have imagined in my wildest fantasy—the incredible surge of excruciating pleasure it would cause. From the first gasping moment—my cock raised, tilted to his lips, sucked in, consumed whole—my senses were overwhelmed and all rational thought and bodily function were lost. I felt myself writhing, clutching, contorting, I heard myself crying out, uttering obscenities interspersed with gibberish, I opened my eyes wide to see nothing, closed them to see the blurring colors of bloodlust, opened them and closed them again, clenching them shut against the onslaught of indescribable agony that wracked my body—an inescapable, unendurable agony that ripped me limb from limb.

For several moments it was as if I had suffered a violent convulsion that gripped my body and held me rigid while my insides erupted, were wrenched away, exploded out of me. Then little by little, the agony abated, sinews released extended limbs, muscles that shone with a film of sweat relaxed, and tension leaving my face ungritted my teeth and eased open the moist lids of my eyes.

"Did you like it?" he asked, lifting his head, swallowing, running his tongue between his lips to collect the dribbles of cum. It was obvious that *he* had; his mile-wide grin was self-congratulatory, lascivious. I smiled through the mist that became droplets in the corners of my eyes. I thought I was going to cry, but to do so made no sense when I felt so supremely fulfilled.

"In America we call that a blow job." His face radiated an ex-patriot's pride.

I giggled, and wished I had not. It seemed like a silly response, immature, and somehow disrespectful. But I was overflowing with an immense happiness. I *felt* silly. I felt lightheaded and frivolous.

"You taste good as you look," he said, tousling my hair, tweaking my nipples, kissing them, kissing the tip of my nose, acting the way I felt; silly, lightheaded, frivolous.

"Did you . . ." I giggled again, embarrassed to ask but dying to know. "Did you swallow it?"

"Every drop," he said, nibbling my chin and then licking it like a cat at a saucer. "And boy, when you let fly you sure shoot a helluva load."

My cheeks flushed and I turned my face away to hide my embarrassment, feeling greatly flattered and faintly revolted. I stared at the tattoo on his swelling biceps while he nuzzled the ear and the side of my neck I had turned to him. A globe and an anchor were a sharply-defined blue on his brown flesh. Beneath the globe was a wavy rectangular banner that could have been flying in a steady breeze, and the words contained in the borders of the banner were a red script:

Semper Fidelis. Under the banner in bolder block letters was USMC.

What he was doing to my neck behind my ear tickled and I was also aware of something hard and cold doing a rhythmless little tap dance on my chest. "What are they?" I asked, turning to face him, touching the two metal disks that dangled loosely from the chain around his neck.

"Dog tags."

I grinned. "You're not a dog."

"No, But I used to get treated like one." His face went stern, tight-lipped.

"Where? Back home, in the States?"

He nodded. "When I was your age."

"Is that why you didn't go back?"

There was no answer. I watched his face and waited, expectant. His body tautened out of its slump and his voice was soft and chiding: "You ask a lotta questions, Captain." Then he laughed a laugh that seemed to put us both at ease.

"What's that written on them?" I was holding the disks so near one rested on the bridge of my nose.

"The story of my life, fella. Or enough anyone'd need to know if they came across the corpse."

"Do you always wear them?" I knew I was asking questions again but I could not stop myself.

"Yep, always. They're the only thing I got that's real. Without these babies I ain't nobody." He stretched out on his side on the floor, resting his belly against me with a leg drawn up across my thighs. I could feel his hard cock pushing into my hip.

If I said I had not really thought about the man's cock, his needs, it would not be the truth. I had thought about him every minute of the day since those brief, horrific, soul-shattering moments by the creek; my orgasm induced by little more than the intimate nearness of his body to mine. And I had thought about doing to him, even as he did it, what he was doing to me, but his preoccupation with my cock—his single-minded pursuit of it—had precluded any possibility of reciprocal gratification. An ill-timed and potentially clumsy attempt on my part to initiate something I knew virtually nothing about could have diminished rather than enhanced our mutual enjoyment of each other. I also thought, I told myself, *you think too much.*

His cock, larger than life (certainly larger than mine), was rubbing hungrily and oozing profusely on my flank. With a quick furtive glance at his face to be sure he was wearing that certain smile and hoping my confidence did not seem too blatantly false, I reached down between our bodies, our hips, trying to act as if it was a casual, everyday thing to do, and took his cock in my hand. Holy Jesus! I was immediately struck by how solid and brute-powerful it was, yet its skin was softly tender, damp, and as smooth as spun silk. I sighed, and he did too, as I wrapped my fingers around its meaty thickness. Beautiful, I thought, now understanding how a cock could be. It's *beautiful!*

I squeezed the man's chunky shaft and worked my fist up and down the length of it from base to broad, stubby head. His body pressed closer to mine, his hips making small thrusts that gently pistoned his cock inside my closed fist. He was moaning and biting into the fleshy part of my shoulder, kissing and biting along my neck to my face. His excitement—that I was its cause—thrilled me. When his leg jerked higher across my hips my cock went hard again under the weight and warmth of the tensing muscles.

Suddenly, his body was on top of me. The weight of him pinioned me to the coarse sacking and I was overwhelmed by feelings of insignificance and supplication. Warned by a tremulous panic in my limbs, I wrapped my arms across his back, clinging to him, clutching his taut flesh with trembling fingers, fearing that I might fall away from him, melt through the loft platform and disappear into a bottomless pit below. The expanse of his broad chest covered mine, urgently bearing down, heaving, and his mouth was on my mouth, forcing my lips apart. His cock, clamped full-length to mine, began a slow, rhythmic shaft-to-shaft frictioning. Pushing his hands down under my body, he gripped my buttocks to draw me closer, tightening our connection so that each thrust of his pelvis ground our hipbones together and forced from my mouth an articulated gasp: "Oh..." And the dog tags bit cruelly into my chest.

His kisses were becoming more passionate, as if to stifle my involuntary cries, and his pushing more rapid, a mutual liquid ooze allowing a lubricious sliding of his cock along mine. Without seeing or even knowing numbers in my head, I counted as though my cock was counting and recording his thrusting assault, counting each slithery, searing attack he made against it. At twenty-two I was suddenly unable to count further, numbers whirling and spinning away like glittering sparks from a catherine wheel, and I was suffering an immense implosion as if every organ in my body was collapsing. I heard myself grunting in the frantic rhythm of his thrusts while I clawed the flesh of his back with my fingers. He shoved against me with the bellowing cry of a stricken animal and at the same time I felt a surge of hot liquid across my belly, not knowing whether it was his orgasm or mine. Or both combined.

Later, when I had extricated myself, wriggling like a slippery eel out from under his inert mass of torso and splayed limbs, I said, "Use this," offering my tee-shirt to wipe down our bodies.

"Will you come back? Tomorrow night," he asked, seriously, when we were cleaned up, tucking my cock into my shorts, buttoning me up as if I was a helpless child.

"Yeah," I said, trying to suppress a smile; his fumbling fingers tickled.

As I cautiously felt with a foot for each rung of the ladder, descending into enveloping darkness, I heard him say to me, to the rafters high overhead, to himself: "Beautiful." And because I thought it and felt it, I said "beautiful," too, but I did not know precisely why.

The air was cool and invigorating on my bare chest as I trotted home, a soggy tee-shirt flapping jauntily from the waistband of my shorts where he had tucked it. In my bedroom, I spread the unsightly remains of my shirt across the pillow, buried my nose in its crumpled dampness, took two slow, chest-expanding breaths, let my smile become a yawn, and slipped into that long deep sleep of growing boys.

* * *

THE FOLLOWING EVENING AT TEA, Dad described the new man's performance in and around the woolshed with more laudation than was customarily given to any employee, no matter how productive. "He might be a bloody Yank," he concluded, slamming down his fork for emphasis, "but the bugger worked like a Trojan."

Unconvinced, Mum said, "I still don't like the looks of him. And he drinks."

"They all bloodywell drink."

"I wouldn't trust him as far as I could kick him. And he's a skite, a smooth talker."

"They all are. Bloody Americans. Schools over there teach 'em that."

"What's he doing over here, anyway? The war ended ten years ago."

"Dunno. It's none of my business. Or bloody yours for that matter," Dad said, ready to argue the point all evening. "Maybe he likes it better here. You can't blame him."

"If you ask me there's something fishy about the whole thing. I could feel it in my bones the minute I set eyes on him."

I was itching to voice my opinion of the new man, trying to project a picture-theatre image in my mind of our stolid meal-table gathering if I should announce: "He sucked my dick and swallowed all the stuff." But the big screen in my brain remained blank, the vision too opaque and improbable to be perceived.

"Please may I be excused," I said, neatly rolling my serviette, threading its mulga wood ring. This was not a request but the accepted announcement of departure; nobody ever responded with a yes or a no. Leaving them still bickering, I sought the companionship of my dog to kill time, to dispose of last night's unsalvageable tee-shirt, to tell him my secrets, having long since discovered that a dog's best friend is an only child.

Three hours and eleven minutes later, I executed a well-planned escape from my bedroom by way of the window. It went without a hitch, except for a small triangular rip in the front of my clean tee-shirt, snagging it on the lock as I lowered myself from the sill. By increasing the size of the tear I found I could effectively and, I thought, provocatively reveal my right nipple, which I kept pinching as I ran to the shed, making it pointed and tingly and fetchingly inflamed. I thought of my exit through the window (I could have more safely and quietly gone through the door) as an intrepid escape from brutalizing captors, initiated by an American Marine who was about to give me, along with more deliciously wicked things, a hero's welcome.

And who was asleep. When I climbed into the loft the lantern was lit, turned low, and sonorous sounds of snoring came from a blanketed shape in the dimness. At first I felt miserable with disappointment that he had not been awake to appreciate my athletic ascent to his aerie, but suspecting that he had not worked as hard as he had done that day for some time, my spirits lifted and a warm, anticipatory stirring in my groin thickened my cock. I slipped off my sandals and tiptoed across the dry, creaking board to the figure reclining in a fetal curve on a mattress of bales and blankets. I stood over him, my pulse quickening with expectation and trespass, and unfastened my shorts, letting them fall to my feet, side-stepping out of them.

Naked from the waist down, feeling more sexual than vulnerable in my torn tee-shirt, I knelt beside him, carefully pulling back a fraying edge of the blanket. He stirred momentarily and the snoring ceased as I continued to gently uncover his body. Reaching out to the lantern, I turned up the crescent of flame to see him better, his body assuming highlights of glowing orange. In admiration and awe I gazed upon the flawless cut and detail of his musculature, his near-perfect physique. Even as he slept, the maleness he exuded, the aura of Pan-like lasciviousness, seemed menacingly potent. Was it this my mother saw that so disturbed her?

Desire drew me closer. I touched his shoulder, lightly, then carefully traced the unfurling outline of the American flag tattooed there, peering closely to decipher the scrolled letters beneath it. Lack of light made the words unreadable, or they might have been in Latin. I lowered my face more to erase a small star with the tip of my tongue. The salty-sweet taste of his skin and the smell of it—sweat, tobacco and whiskey—repelled and excited me. My senses keenly aroused, I kissed the dampened star, inhaling him, tasting him for repletion. Then I kissed the star next to it, and the one next to that, and another, and the next until his shoulder was sheened with saliva and my cock was erect, its protuberance draped with folds of tee-shirt, its tumescent head leaking viscous liquid strands to the floorboards.

He groaned and mumbled something and his sleeping became fitful. An arm struck out, a leg kicked, retracted slowly then kicked again, his head moved from side to side. In spasmodic fits and starts he rolled onto his back, unfolding, splaying out limbs like spokes of a wheel. Holding my nagging erection in my hand, I sat back on my haunches to look at this enigmatic stranger, to let my eyes wander the flung-out, naked body of a man I already knew intimately yet did not know at all. In his presence I felt humbled and exalted, realizing the emergence of my sexual self; not a transformation, but a cognizance of myself as a man who loved men. I shuddered in the heavy stillness and listened to our breathing.

Needing to confirm the warmth, the reality of his body, I placed the flat of my hand on his rippled, concave belly. The muscles contracted and relaxed against my palm. I circled my hand, feeling the heat and resiliency of his flesh, then hesitantly, I reached further to brush the satiny skin of his plump, tubular cock with my fingers. Its response was immediate: it quivered and rolled into the valley of his groin as if to avoid inquisitive fingers by being coy and elusive. In playful pursuit, I pounced on it and coiled my first around its huge girth, applying a gentle pressure of rebuke. Captured, with no possible chance of escape, its proportions began to increase rapidly, swelling, lengthening, extending itself in my grasp. I watched in awe as my clenched fingers were forced apart, no longer able to close around its incredible thickness. I stroked it luxuriously, amazed at the power it generated, and the man moaned as though being subjected to exquisite torture. Spurred on by his response, by my own driven lust, I fisted the now-rigid shaft with determination and delight, fascinated by the excess skin that rolled back and forth over the flaring, dark-purple head at my every stroke.

With his drooling, blood-engorged cock in my right hand and mine in my left, I set about a rhythmic pumping of each, pursuing it for what I hoped would be an eternity of mounting pleasure. But the melting and scalding sensations in my loins quickly increased, becoming unendurable. I was whipped into a frenzy of flashing fists that caused something to explode at the root of my being, forcing a churning, unbearable pressure upward from inside, bursting out, leaping uncontrollably from me. Stream after stream of ejected seed spattered across his belly, forming pooled shapes of brilliant whiteness. Even as I gasped for life, the intensity of my spurting not yet diminished, his own ejaculation began.

I felt the rush of hot, creamy fluid on my face, splashing my cheeks, my nose, my parted lips. I jerked back, tasting the bittersweet tang of his semen, watching each successive burst expand the puddled wash of cum on his belly. When he was finally spent I fondled his cock, squeezing its spongy shaft as it grew limp to coax out the remaining droplets. I dabbled in the sea of cum with both hands, smearing it sensuously across his chest, pinching his nipples into slickened, sticky points, anointing the flag on his shoulder, kissing again the filmed and blurry stars until they shone as brightly as before. With a cum-coated palm I greased my cock and the thought and slippage of our combined juices made me hard again.

I let myself sink into a half-sleep of contentment, certain that this man would be a part of my life forever. A violent spasm in his body brought me back to lucidity, ungluing my cheek from his belly where it had sagged in cummy bliss. I jerked upright to sitting and so did he, letting out a piercing, anguished cry that dislodged a flurry of nesting swallows from the ridge beams. His eyes were open, wide open and glazed with terror, looking at me but not seeing. Recognition came as his surroundings slowly registered.

"Fuck, fella," he said, panting, his forehead beaded with sweat, "I was back on the island . . . that hell-hole in the Pacific . . . enjoying the hospitality of the Japs . . ." He paused to breathe deeply, then added with a cracked, mirthless laugh, "They was serving us bayoneted guts for breakfast."

"You were a prisoner?"

For a long time he was silent, as if remembering or trying not to remember. I watched a tiny muscle or vein near his temple, throbbing, throbbing. "I was a lotta things," he said, "but nothing to worry your pretty head about." Then he laughed his easy laugh. I was not sure that I liked being called pretty, but when he took my arm I let myself be pulled down on top of him.

"C'mon here, you sexy young bastard," he growled, bringing his hands to either side of my face and kissing me full on the mouth. My cheeks flushed wildly and there were palpitations, urgent flutterings in my heart and in my groin. With his mouth still locked to mine, tongues intertwining, he rolled us over so that I was beneath him; his hands spreading fire wherever they traveled, igniting me in ways I would never have thought possible. He stripped the tee-shirt over my head, then, starting at my cum-smudged cheek, he licked and sucked his way down the entire length of my body, lingering at points of passage that were so extraordinarily sensitive to his suctioning lips and delving tongue I writhed to escape the fierce pleasure they caused there; my armpits, each tender, budlike nipple, my navel, the tapering inguinal planes of my belly, the musky depth between my buttocks, the hidden nooks and crannies of my toes.

I squirmed and groaned and whispered, I bucked and whimpered and called out, shouting, crying out my rapture without ever uttering a single cogent word. He tongued his way from my toes to my balls and sucked each one in turn into his mouth, chewing and rolling and squeezing them until I grunted with pain. The moment his lips hotly circled the rim of my glans, the quickening build to climax began. Knowing this, he plunged his mouth down over my cock, forcing its swollen head to the back of his constricted throat. And he kept it there, lodged deeply, massaged by membrane and muscle, for the duration of my ejaculation.

That night, I experienced the gamut of wanton pleasure; a whirlwind trip around the world of sex and back again. He could not seem to get enough of me. Looking at, caressing, kissing my nearly fleshed-out, almost hairless adolescent body with its smooth and pale-honeyed skin kept him in a constant state of arousal. He reveled in my uninhibited naïveté, my earthy innocence, my raw-boned, young-muscled vigor. He nurtured and was delighted by my insatiable curiosity for all things sexual. He worshipped my robust, country-boy cock, and he loved—could not *ever* get enough of—my cum. The seemingly inexhaustible supply of youthfresh semen from my full-hanging, rareripe balls was nectar to him; delectable, life-sustaining stuff that he sought, fought for, and savored to the very last seeping smidgen. And I was always eager, able and ever-ready to give succor.

For two weeks and two days, from ten until midnight every evening, I escaped form my cruel captors—by way of the door after three nights of ripped tee-shirts—to seek salvation in the arms of my mysterious stranger. Often, when I was in a skittish mood, I would undress in the shed and announce my arrival from the top of the ladder with a naked, hard-cocked salute:

"Your horny young stud, sir. Reporting for a blow job, *sir!*"

I sincerely believed our two-hour-a-day-together life would endure all adversities and last forever. My dog inside the house was the first inkling I had that our affair had come to an end.

No animals, even pets, were allowed in our house. When we returned from church that Sunday afternoon to find the screen door unlatched, standing open, and myriad flies and my dog in happy cohabitation in the kitchen, I knew something was amiss. Sometimes I would take my dog with us to the small granite church twelve miles away where the district minister held a noon service on the second Sunday of every month. My dog would amuse himself chasing rabbits from the overgrown blackberry bushes in the churchyard and pissing on the headstones, which, as most of these were our relatives, I regarded as all-in-the-family urinations of exuberance rather than disrespect. But that Sunday we had not taken him and now there he was, thumping his tail on the cool linoleum in Mum's kitchen.

A sack of flour had been nosed over in the pantry, nothing more serious. I gave my dog a friendly kick in the rump and scooted him out onto the veranda while Dad straightened up the pantry and Mum went to their bedroom to change out of her Sunday best. A high-pitched shriek sent Dad and me running down the hall to investigate. Their room was a shambles. Wardrobe doors yawned open, dressing-table drawers were hanging out and clothes were strewn everywhere; nothing a dog would want to do, or know how to if he did.

Searching and sorting revealed that a silver-backed hand mirror was missing, as was an heirloom cameo brooch that had belonged to my great-grandmother. With another bloodcurdling cry Mum saw that the sable stole she had worn on their honeymoon to the Blue Mountains was gone. Certain items of jewelry were not to be found: an opal ring, two ropes of pearls, one real, one simulated, and a sapphire pendant Dad had given her on their wedding anniversary.

"I told you, didn't I? I told you I didn't like the looks of him," Mum said smugly when Dad came back from the shed to report that there was no sign of the hired man or his belongings.

That he was gone, that he had left me without a word, a warning, a goodbye, anything, seemed inconceivable to me. I ran to the shed, clambered to the loft, shouting, "Where are you? Where are you?" Everything was as it was before he came. There was nothing to indicate that he had ever been there at all. Nothing, except four whiskey bottles lined up in tight formation, meticulously placed, like soldiers on parade frozen for inspection. I stood, likewise frozen, and the first bitter tears I would shed in the name of love streamed down my cheeks.

In my room, later, when the commotion had died down, I stood by the window and watched the setting sun and the bats darting like spectral shapes in a fiery sky. I stood until the sky was inky black, then turning away, I noticed the lid was off the small wooden box on my chest of drawers where I kept the money given to me for birthdays and at Christmas. Counting it regularly, I knew I had fifteen pounds, twelve shillings and sixpence saved toward a new bicycle. The money was gone.

When I looked more closely I saw that the box was not empty. At the very bottom, blending in with the darkly stained interior, there was what appeared to be a scattering of tiny metallic objects. I turned the box over to tip them into my hand and with a soft whooshing sound a chain slid into my palm, a chain threaded with two metal disks each identically stamped with a row of numbers, a religion, a blood type, and a name I would never forget.

* * *

LOOKING BACK OVER MY LIFE, I sometimes see myself, young and strong and willful on those summer nights, when I was tempted, touched and first loved by a mysterious stranger. There is much of him—and yes, the dog tags—I still wear today.

Lucky in Love

I WALKED OUT of the little corner shop at the north end of Bondi Beach into the fresh, salt-sharp air. Barefoot and bare-chested. "I think I'm in love," I was saying to myself. "In love for the first bloody time in my life." Wanting to be, but not wanting to believe it. The bell rang inside the shop as the door closed behind me and the early morning sun, glinting across the glassy expanse of ocean, hit me right in the eyes. There was no heat to it yet but I could tell the day was going to be a scorcher. And there would be no surf worth a damn.

He was on my mattress, asleep, when I came back with the eggs, bread and milk. He grunted, rolled over and grinned at me. For some reason he looked insecure, apprehensive, probably not sure if I was going to make breakfast for the two of us. Or just for myself. Not sure if he ought to be there at all, the morning after.

"Want some grub, big boy?" I said, to put his mind at rest, not liking the looks of him in daylight nearly as much as I did by last night's candleglow. But that's not unusual, you say.

"Too right." His grin got bigger and he looked more sure of himself. Almost cocky. "Fuckin makes me fuckin hungry," he said, scratching the reddish-gold patch around his fat, floppy cock, laughing like an unclogged drain.

"You and me both, mate." I dumped the stuff on the table and started sorting it out. "Ta," I said when he lit two smokes and threw me one.

I cracked six eggs into a bowl, poured in some milk, and watched him blowing thin streams of smoke into the air as I whisked with a canny wrist. I had to admit to myself he was more funny-looking than good-looking. His wild and woolly thatch of carrot-colored hair looked as if a lawnmower had run amok through it. His eyes were shifty, animal-alert and set wide apart in a squarish face that was irregularly freckled but without that pale pink-orange complexion most red-headed boys have. With a low chunky forehead and semaphore ears at temple height, he reminded me vaguely of a throwback to earlier times. His nose being slightly off-center where something or someone had broken it didn't help matters. Or did, if symmetry in a face isn't to your liking.

I remembered last night, standing face to face to strip off what little we had on, that he wasn't tall—his head only came up to my nose—but he was broad and thickset and strong as an ox. I liked him then and I liked our screwing later; he was a slow starter, but once I'd got him revved up he had a savage approach to fucking which I specially liked. We must've been at it until near four o'clock, drinking beer, smoking, talking, and fucking. It was nearly four, I know, when I told him I loved him. I'd just come for the umpteenth time and my dick was soft and squishy inside him. We were both a bit drunk, and when I told him we both blubbered like babies. I wasn't sure now, beating eggs, if I knew what love was. If I ever did know. I blew dust and a dead cockroach out of my frying pan and lit the gas.

When I came home from work yesterday I found him sitting outside my place, outside on the concrete steps to the blocks of flats where I rent. The place is a dump but dirt cheap and only three short streets from the beach. Not exactly the Hotel Australia, though nor is the price. I would've walked right past that sprawled-out jaunty toughboy but there was something about his poorly acted arrogance that held me on the steps halfway. A lost-puppy look. A sad-eyed all-forlorn hopelessness that sent signals down my spine and made my dick sit up and take notice.

He said he had nowhere to go. No job, no money, no nothing. Around here I see plenty like him. Fucked-up, fucked-over kids who come down from the country, kids who'd never had anything and never would. They are the flotsam and jetsam, life-forsaken dregs of humanity who end up in the city looking for something they wouldn't recognize if they fell over it. All I wanted from him, I said, was to fuck him. I told him that and he followed me inside anyway.

Corcoran, he said his name was, something Corcoran, which I didn't catch because with his kind names don't mean anything. A good fuck was all I was interested in; he was hardly worth much else. I told him that, too. He didn't mind me saying so, he'd heard it said many a time before. Inside, he was more than friendly, more than willing; he did everything I asked him to do and liked, or pretended to like, doing it.

"Corker is what they call me," he said, so Corker—when I called him anything—was what I called him. He was easy to read; he needed company, someone to talk to, to listen mainly. When we weren't fucking he was talking. I dropped a big dollop of bacon grease in the pan and when it sputtered into a smoky liquid I slid in the egg mixture.

Corker told me he'd hitchhiked from some shitty little tin-pot town in South Australia and got arrested two days later in Victoria. They let him out of jail when they checked back by phone with somebody at the reform school and discovered he really was eighteen years old and had been officially released. He'd been telling them that all along, from the moment they'd picked him up in the public lavatory where he was getting his dick sucked by some toothless old fart for ten bob.

I didn't bother to ask about his parents or relatives because there probably weren't any. Any who gave a fuck one way or the other, that is. I didn't ask him about anything because I suppose I didn't give a fuck either. Not at first. But that didn't stop him telling. His mouth was going a mile a minute, until I put my cock to him. Then, to give him credit, he shut his trap and opened his legs and took my rod like a trooper. That dopey kid certainly knew how to fuck.

"Fuckin oath, that smells good," he said to me as I prodded the steaming yellow gunk in the pan. I was hoping it'd taste better than it looked because it looked like monkey shit.

"When didya eat last?" I put a teaspoon of instant coffee into my mug—the only one I had—and another into a glass jar, after I emptied out the nails.

"Dunno. Monday or Tuesday, I reckon."

"Shit fella, it's Friday. You must be fuckin starving." I poured boiling water and milk, and scraped half of the eggs onto my plate and left half in the frying pan. I squatted down on the floor by the mattress and gave him the plate and the mug. My plate, my mug. I felt sorry for him, felt suddenly protective, things I didn't expect to feel. Didn't want to feel.

"I'm orright," he said, looking down at the plate and the mug. "Don't worry about me."

"Who's fuckin worried?" I snapped, angry that he thought I cared. "Y'think I give a rat's ass?" Immediately regretting those jerked-out words.

Silenced, he ate without raising his head, and for some reason I felt like a clumsy idiot, an insensitive moron. I sat there watching him, feeling like a lump of shit. Shitty and depressed. And that's unusual for me because I've got a reputation with the blokes at work and with my surfer mates for being easy-going, devil-may-care, always good for a laugh and a bit of fun. That's how I got called Lucky—happy-go-lucky, see.

When Corker's plate was empty he still didn't lift his eyes. I gave him more slices of bread and a jar I found that had some Vegemite left in it. He ate with single-minded determination while I watched, racking my brains for easy conversation. I tossed the rest of the loaf on the mattress beside him and picked up the empty Vegemite jar which he'd wiped out clean with a licked finger. I wanted to say something to him, something nice that would let him know I wasn't angry anymore, something encouraging, personal. I wanted to explain to him how I'd once experienced what he was going through, that I understood, but I couldn't seem to find the right words so I made him another mug of coffee.

"Ta," he said, glancing up at me, lifting his face enough for me to see the wet streaks on his cheeks. He'd eaten everything I'd given him including the entire loaf of bread, minus three pieces I'd taken for myself. And speaking of me, I haven't said much about yours truly, you say. There's not really much to report on that subject. I'm six years older than Corker which, if you can add right, makes me twenty-four. Born to a share farmer, I was the youngest of eight kids so when I left home at fourteen they all breathed a big sigh of relief. I never was a handsome brute like most of my brothers, but I was built better. I work now because I want to; to put proper food in my gut, to keep out of arm's reach of the law, to have a place of my own, and most important, to keep some self-respect. I take jobs on building sites mostly—it's hard yakker but the pay's decent, and nobody asks questions. Like all Aussie builders' laborers I do the job in short shorts and big boots. I'm proud of my body and enjoy showing it off. When they don't call me Lucky, they call me Tarzan, and when I'm not working I'm surfing, in the pub with the lads, or fucking. That's it about me. Short and sweet.

Corker upended his coffee mug and looked at me, really *looked* at me, as if he was seeing me for the first time as a person, as if he could see everything inside. It made me edgy, a bit nervous.

"Y'do this much?" he asked. His voice was quiet, his face serious.

"Do what?" Then, "Thanks, mate," I said, taking the cigarette he was handing me.

"Y'know... I mean, fuck around like this... with blokes?" For once I didn't have a ready answer. It wasn't a question I'd been asked before. Ever. I kept thinking I ought to be pissed off, him asking like that—bold as brass—a personal thing he had no business asking about. But for some reason I wasn't angry, I was pleased, sort of flattered, as if he was paying me a compliment. The expression on his tense face told me it wasn't a casual question. He needed an answer, he needed to know for his own self. His own piece of mind.

"Yeah, I spose... pretty much," I said. And trying to lighten him up, I added with a cheeky grin, "But I'm real picky." Then, remembering the word, "Fastidious, is what I am."

He laughed his creaky drain-gurgle laugh and I knew right away I liked him more than many of the others. I didn't know why, just that I did. And I knew I could help him, love him, if he'd let me.

"What about girls?" he asked, after a long and thoughtful drag on his cigarette. Dead serious again.

"What about 'em?" I was still in my teasing mood.

"Do ya do it with them, like ya do it with blokes?"

"Fuck 'em, ya mean?"

"Yeah..." It was my guess that he'd never asked these questions before, never had anyone he *could* ask.

"Shit, mate, I'll fuck anything with hair, fluff, fur or feathers between its legs. I've already had a go at the bloody barber's floor. Jesus, when I was your age it was me ambition to fuck meself to death before I hit twenty."

"I'm serious..." he said, but he was smiling. "Do ya fuck girls?" His silly grin was like sunshine.

"Used to, mate. Gave it up as a bad joke." Then, more to myself I said, "Don't know why, but for some reason I could never take to it."

"Me neither." I heard him say as he rolled over to the far edge of the mattress to give me room, to let me know I was welcome. Accepting his invitation, I stretched out beside him, his funny, crooked nose and freckled cheeks only inches from my face. As I reached for the stubby cigarette end that hung loosely between his lips he took my hand and brought it to his chest. I trailed my fingers across its curves and he breathed in deeply, his ribcage swelling, and out again slowly with a sustained sigh of release. With his mind now at ease his body craved relaxation and pleasure.

His nipples were deep-pink, small and perfectly shaped, and each sat bold and high on its hill of muscle. I touched each one in turn, lightly flicking their fleshy points, circling them, and pinching them gently between my thumb and finger. And listened to his contented sighing.

"How about you?" I asked. "Did ya do it with me last night coz ya wanted to or coz ya'd got nowhere else t'go?" Now I was the serious one.

"Bit of both, I spose." He laughed his laugh that bounced his big frame and sent happy vibrations right down to my cock. "I'm glad I did, though," he said, putting his hand on my hard dick, rubbing it up and down through my shorts.

"Do people know... I mean, know that ya mess round with guys?"

"Fuck, no!" I was going to say my surfer mates and the blokes on the building site wouldn't believe it if I did tell them, not in a million years they wouldn't. Me? Tarzan? God's gift to women. The fuck-crazy stud they all wanted to be like. Me? Shit, no! Tell that to the bloody marines. I was going to say that, but Corker was busy undoing my shorts, unzipping them and pulling them down to get at my cock, so I said nothing and let him do what he wanted to do. What we both wanted him to do.

His warm, raspy tongue, running up and down the length of my cock, made me all shivery. I shivered and moaned, "Oh, fuck, yeah," when he took its head into his mouth and started sucking on it. He sucked it—just the head—with loving care, as if there was nothing else on his mind.

Corker understood cock. It was obvious he loved it as much as I did. If he didn't know anything else, he knew a man's cock was himself. He knew that a dick was a bloke's life; his body, his cock, was what he was. It had to be. Corker didn't know much, but he knew that. My cock was throbbing and jumping for joy between his busy lips, when suddenly he disconnected, lifted his face. His cheeks were flushed and motley, his eyelids droopy with risen lust. "It's not just this... your cock... I like..." His gaping mouth was a wet radius; saliva trickled away from its tangents. "It's *you*... I mean, it's everything about ya... everything y'are..." In gentle appreciation I reached down and stroked his hair. It felt nice, moist and springy, not limp.

"Yeah, mate. I like you, too." I wanted to say more, to explain my perception of love, of how I would love him, how we would love each other. I struggled with thoughts and words but couldn't find a way to put them together, couldn't even begin to find a way. So instead of waxing philosophical I touched his damp forehead and watched the funny way his Adam's apple bobbed up and down as he spoke.

"Last night... I was scared shitless when I first come inside, not knowin' what to expect, what you'd be into. Since I come down here, I've run across some pretty weird blokes, had to do some pretty weird things. But with you . . . it was different. Different from them others. After a while I felt good. Sort of safe. Almost happy, ya might say. I reckon it was the first time I done things with a bloke an' never felt alone . . . never felt lonely afterwards."

"You're shitting me," I gibed, when I saw him biting his bottom lip, fighting back tears. If there's one thing I can't stomach, don't know how to handle, is a grown man getting all soppy and bleary-eyed on me. I mean that's exactly what I couldn't stand about screwing sheilas; all their billing and cooing, sniveling and dabbing red eyes with hankies. All that lovey-dovey bullshit makes me sick.

"Last night," he snuffled, pulling himself together, wiping the back of his hand across his runny noise. "Last night was like . . . well, like ya liked what ya was doin' t'me, but ya like *me* as well. Ya made me feel like *someone.* Ya made me like *myself.* I been fucked before, but this was the first time I ever felt good about it afterwards."

"Crikey, Corker . . ." This rough-cut country kid certainly had a way with words, certainly knew how to touch a bloke's heart. Right at that moment I had so much love for him I ached with it. "Corker . . . Corker . . ." I mumbled, annoyed by the lump that had built in my throat and the sudden stinging in my eyes. I gripped his shoulders roughly, rougher than I'd meant to, and pulled him across my body, crushing my mouth to his, my human self responding to the warm and velvety chewing of our lips and tongues. "Corker . . ." I was gasping, "Jesus, Corker . . . I want you," gasping the words into his open mouth, into his heart and soul, "Corker . . . Jesus, I want you."

We were pulled apart finally, not for oxygen, but for my need to see the flesh and bone and muscle of what I was feeling. Kneeling astride his legs, I let my eyes soak up the rugged beauty of his body. My hands, hungry for him, outlined each contour, each resilient curve, modeling him beneath me with meticulous care the way a kid on the beach—paying no attention to other kids around him or the incoming tide—might shape a figure out of sand.

I sucked his nipples, nipping them with my teeth, making them red and swollen. I wet the tips of my fingers and twisted each tiny point, pinching and twisting until he yelped like a puppy and pleaded with me to stop. His rough hands groped and found my cock and stroked it with more energy than expertise. Ready for bigger and better things, I knee-walked back between his legs until the broad meaty head of his ten-incher came into view. I could have sworn it was smiling at me, and as I kissed its tiny mouth a spurt of clear juice slipped out; a hint I knew of the torrent that must be waiting in those big swinging sacs below. I caught that glinting jewel on the very end of my tongue and curled it into my mouth. His sweet secretion was like distilled sunshine with a nutty aftertaste.

Crouching low, I lapped the extravagant length of his weapon from crinkly cock hair to drooling cock knob, top, bottom and both sides. I tongued the bloated head, fucking my pointy tip into the cum slit, then slurped noisily back down the spit-glazed shaft to his balls. When I'm doing a horny young stud like Corker I like it even more if there's something to listen to. Loud sucking and slurpings, lots of moaning and groaning; the sound of good hot sex really turns me on. I was producing plenty of slurp and suck noises and he was responding with enough moans and groans to loosen the plaster off the ceiling. That was another thing I liked about Corker, he was one of the noisiest blokes I'd had the pleasure to get down and dirty with. I could have loved him for that alone.

As a nice long fuck was foremost in my mind, I shifted my attention to lower regions. My fingers sneaked down between his beefy thighs, hovering over his other, tighter-lipped mouth. The little slit puckered its lips, flexed its muscle to let me know it was ready to gobble up anything I had a mind to feed it. Two joints of an obliging finger pushed in and poked about, and the muscle tightened around them with ruthless greed.

"Yes, yes, yesss..." he hissed. "Yes, please, yesss...for crissakes...fuck me."

Corker was panting, primed and hot to trot. As I lowered my hips he hoisted his chunky thighs, lifting and spreading them wide, clamping them across my back, locking his ankles tight to my ass cheeks. Our bodies seemed to automatically adjust their tilt and alignment, repositioning to connect my aggressor cock to his sweet-lipped, oh-so-fuckable asshole. I could feel his heartbeat through the nub of my dick. I pushed a bit, enough to get myself just barely inside, and paused there long enough to drive him mad for more.

"Oh, fuck me . . . please, fuck me . . ." he pleaded. With a long deep sigh and a long deep thrust, I gave him everything I had. Penetration was easy, direct and uncomplicated. I felt myself sucked in, swallowed down into warm and accepting softness, felt the slow conquering descent into gripping membranes of heat and wetness and raw energy. Powerful pulling hands on my ass cheeks sank me deeper still until I hit rock bottom, then the inevitable nerve-wracking piston strokes of fucking took control.

"Fuck me . . . fuck me . . . fuck me . . ." he moaned, and I was only too happy to oblige. I pumped into him like I was steam driven, plunging harder and deeper with each stroke. My balls slapped against him with a wet heavy sound as I buried myself to the root again and again. He squirmed and wriggled his bum beneath me, huffing and puffing his approval. The muscle-lined walls of his asshole gripped my pistoning cock like a bruiser's brute fist. His tight little fuckhole was proving to be all I'd hoped for and more. I couldn't help thinking my curving cock fit Corker's streamlined ass like they'd been made for each other in Heaven. A good fuck always makes me think romantic thoughts.

I wanted this fuck to last a good long time so I steadied down to a nice easy rhythm. I began by giving him slow-motion all-the-way-in all-the-way-out passes that did great things for my dick but were not severe enough to make me blow my stack. I could fuck all night at that speed if I had to. After a while I shifted gears for something a bit different. Variety is the spice of life, they say. I pulled out my slippery stalk until only its fat knob was inside, then drove it home slowly, real slow and careful, into Corker's cock-starved channel. I pulled out quickly and went back very slowly, repeating this action over and over. Corker was loving it. His talented asshole clutched and squeezed and did all sorts of clever things to my cudgel.

The next variation was to reverse what I'd just been doing. I withdrew at a snail's pace, paused at the steamy entrance to his fuckhole, and harpooned his quivering guts with a swift and deadly downstroke. Each time I rammed myself into him, Corker let out a yell like a stuck pig. His yelling and cursing and babbling was so intense that if you'd been listening outside my door you'd have thought I was entertaining a stark raving loony. The poor bloke was whipped into a frenzy. "Fuckin Jesus, I gotta cum," he groaned, but each time he reached for his bouncing cock to whack himself off, I knocked his hand away.

"Let me cum," he pleaded, "Please, let me cum . . . please . . . I gotta . . ."

"You'll cum when I cum," I growled through gritted teeth, increasing tempo, shifting into top gear, gaining speed and force. Closing in for the kill.

Looking down between our sweaty bodies, I saw Corker's monster cock bucking uncontrollably, its head inflamed a bright purply-red and swollen ready to burst. I knew it would be only a matter of seconds before he let go his load. And a few seconds was all I needed because the time was right for me too. I ground my cock into his upturned humping ass and made a series of lightning-speed thrusts that took his breath away and took me over the edge.

"I'm fuckin coming," I growled. "I'm gonna come in yer fuckin ass."

"Fuckin give it t'me," he cried. "Gimme yer fuckin load."

With a final thrust I drove my exploding weapon to the hilt, shooting my wad deep into his gut.

"Oooh, fuckin Jesus, I'm coming . . ." As my cum squirted into him, Corker's frantic cries became louder and a ropy chain of thick cream shot from his gaping cock slit. He unleashed stream after stream of hot cum that splashed my chest and dripped down onto his. Crying out and cursing and holding onto each other for dear life, we let go our big loads together. And we kept holding on, choking for air, as our cocks' fierce squirting became a slow seep.

After unloading, we fell back in a heap, more or less comatose. And later, pulling my soft sticky dick out of him, I asked, "How's yer bumhole feel?"

"Hmmm, just beaut, mate," he purred, like a satisfied tomcat. "Feels full as a tick." And so saying he flashed me a gappy-toothed grin, rolled onto his back, closed his eyes, and went out like a light. Activity in the street outside and the angle of the sun told me it was time I got ready for work. I sauntered into the kitchen for a shit, shave and shower. My bathroom and kitchen are one and the same, and don't ask me how. You wouldn't believe it if I told you.

Dousing warm sudsy water on my chest, watching the thick globs of cum wash down my belly like busy little wriggling grubs, I let my mind meander aimlessly the way it likes to do after a good early morning fuck. In the pit-a-pat spray and steam, it idled happily through recent events until it bumped into Corker, and me being in love. There it balked. Stopped dead in its tracks. It always did on that subject because that's what I'd trained it to do. The training was part of my program for self-preservation, for staying a whole fucked-up person. Most people, I'd reckoned, tried to analyze love too much when they were in it. They tried to make it make sense, make it fit the shape of their lives. But it doesn't make sense and it won't be shaped. Even the word *love* sounds like nothing when you start saying it too much. Fucking to love and loving to fuck is my motto.

Or it was, up until then. Up until I ran across Corker. That dumb-shit dopey kid somehow meant a lot more to me than just a lively fuckmate. Don't ask me why. I don't analyze, remember. So, turning off the water and my mind, I toweled down, filled up the kettle and lit the gas. I fluffed up the fuzz around my dick with a mostly toothless comb while waiting for the water to boil. I like to see my dick hair looking neat and tidy.

When I brought in the coffee Corker had two cigarettes lit in his hand. I exchanged the mug for one of them, and said, "Get that into ya and ya'll feel like a new man." He'd been sleeping for fifteen, twenty minutes at the most and looked like someone had been rabbit-punching him the whole time. Corker was no beauty at the best of times.

"I smell worsen a fuckin bag fulla rotten mangoes," he grimaced, alternating between sipping his coffee and sniffing his shaggy armpits.

"No one's complaining," I said. "If ya wanna have a wash there's a shower in there." I nodded toward the kitchen.

"Yeah, mate. Don't mind if I do." He upended his mug and handed it back to me. I wasn't sure whether that was his way of being polite or whether he regarded me as room service. I gave him a sideways scowl and the benefit of the doubt.

"Try not t'leave any dick hairs on me soap," I said, being fussy about things like that.

"Righty-o, mate. I gotta use yer thunderbox first, but."

Gathering up the breakfast things I followed him into the kitchen, admiring his humpy melon-shaped ass. I had to fight back a mad urge to sink my teeth into those yummy globes. Corker settled himself on the crapper with a faraway look on his face while I rinsed the plate, mug and the glass jar under the cold tap. If I'd used the hot water Corker's shower would've run cold. I was about to put the nails back in the jar when the possibility of tomorrow's breakfast occurred to me. I put the jar next to my mug on the shelf.

"You're outa shit paper," he said, looking embarrassed to have to say so. It's always struck me as peculiar how blokes can be happy as a lark to take your cock up their bum, but when it comes to taking a shit out of the same hole they're overcome with acute coyness.

"Ya should be fulla cum, not shit," I said snidely, tearing up the grocery bag. "Here dickface, try this for size. Might be a tad rough on yer tender fuckhole though."

"Watcha call this then?" he giggled. "Cum paper?" He winced as he applied it to his rear end. Then laughed. His laughter was infectious; I started too.

While Corker, warbling tunelessly under the shower nozzle, scraped away at his Greek-god-like bod, I scraped away at the crud-encrusted frying pan. Cold water wasn't interested in dissolving what was cooked into it. Giving up in disgust, I said, "Fuck the bloody frying pan." And Corker turned off the shower.

"Ya can fuck me instead," he chortled, whipping aside the plastic curtain. For a moment I thought he was joking, but when he stuck out his watery bum and parted his asscheeks to rudely display his delectable little pink-puckered hole, I knew my kitchen duties were far from over and done with.

Moving nearer for a close-up inspection, I caught a whiff of him, all zesty-clean and soapy-fresh and exuding appetizing smells. I nuzzled his neck and stroked his shoulders, scattering crystal-like droplets of water. I stroked the broad sweep of his back down to the expandingly beautiful cheeks of his firm cushiony ass, lingering at the artfully exposed little hole circled in damp amber ringlets. I stroked down his sturdy muscular thighs to his equally sturdy and bulging calves. With my body curved over, bent to the exact shape of his, I gave in to my earlier mad urge and bit lustfully into the peach-ripe flesh of his asscheeks. Radical thoughts and darkly exotic intentions raced through my mind. Billowing waves of excitement surged and crested as I buried my face into the fragrant valley of those full-fruited mounds. I prodded the softening, loosening lips of his asshole with my tongue, breathing in the tangy spices that wafted out of the mysterious crevice. It was enough to boggle the mind.

My cock had quickly reached its fully erect proportions in unaided shuddering jerks, anxious to replace my probing tongue in Corker's willing and wanting, juiced-up cavity. At the best of times my cock is egotistical, self-centered and downright pig-headed, but whatever nasty characteristics it possesses when off duty, hanging low, they are ten times worse when it is in an upstanding state of fuck-ready arousal. When it comes to fucking, I don't fuck around with my cock.

"Shit, mate, ain't ya gonna stick it in?" Corker was just as impatient as my dick. He seemed to have developed a chronic addiction for my uninhibited member. "C'mon, mate, put that fuckin big thing inta me," he said, a bit peevishly, widening his stance on the wet tiles and bracing himself with two hands on the wall in readiness. Not a lad to be easily intimidated by a cranky uptight dong, Corker was nonetheless woefully unprepared for my agitated cock's ungentlemanly approach to the intimate act of anal entry. At crucial moments like this my cock could be a real prick. When I pointed its ill-mannered head at his back door—already unlatched and invitingly ajar—it shoved in without bothering to knock or a beg-your-pardon. All of it, shoulder, shaft and thickening root, was deeply and deftly inserted to a yelp of assaulted surprise from a host who hadn't expected to receive his oversized guest in one fell swoop.

"Holy fucking Jesus fucking Christ." Or words to that effect were Corker's cried-out welcome.

"Easy, young-fella-me-lad. Easy, boy," I murmured in his ear, stroking his wet flanks to steady him down. It was very important for me to get him to relax the constricted muscle that was threatening to nip my dick off at the base. "Easy there, boy. Easy does it."

Corker's tense-tight pucker let go bit by bit, and when he was finally calm and collected, when he wriggled his bottom and gladly accepted his lot, the accommodations greatly improved.

"Christ, mate," he said over his shoulder, "what didja shove up me—a fuckin telephone pole?" His raspy voice had a nice blend of complaint and awestruck wonder.

My snugly held cock, always happy to get some praise and respect and now finding the premises exactly to its liking, settled in for some serious fucking. The action was a bit rough and ready at first; he kept skidding and losing his foothold on the scummy tilework; I was unnecessarily intrepid in charting unexplored territory. But soon we harmonized into a mutually rewarding rhythm of long pithy pushing-and-pulling, a gutsy give-and-take that got us gurgling in appreciation.

Pushed past the fiery edge of self-control, hopelessly het up and relentlessly driven, my ramrodding cock followed a frenzied will of its own. The onrushing stampede could only be checked when all its feverish frantic need was satisfied, when all the pent-up boiling fluids, exploding under pressure, were expelled, spat out, blown away.

"Oh, fuckin sweet Jesus . . ." I gasped. "I'm coming."

"Shoot it inta me. Shoot it! Shoot it!" Corker reached frantically between my legs and grabbed my bouncing balls in one big fist, squeezing out rich syrupy circuits of cum that flowed through my cock and gushed in creamy spurts into his greedy ass-depths.

"Shoot it . . . shoot it . . . shoot it . . ." he chanted as his own thick gobs of cum came squirting out, spat-splatting on the tiles in sporadic bursts, forming splotchy liquid ovals on the glazed ceramic squares.

We sagged slowly to the shower floor, arms and legs all over the place, flopping about uselessly like a two-headed octopus in its death throes. We fought for our lives, for the air to sustain us, and with our bodies locked into each other, our hearts and minds battling to be understood, we fought for our love. Jesus we did. In that unlikely arena, that small rectangle of pitted and mildew-stained tile, we fought the final round and, slipping and scrabbling to extricate crushed limbs, we conceded points, threw in the towel and called it a draw.

"I love you." I meant it. Oh Christ how I meant it. But I couldn't say it. Somehow, in sober daylight, the words seemed only like words; silly-sounding and empty and stripped of any meaning. Struggling to take each other's weight, lifting an arm, supporting a shoulder—more hindrance than help—we brought ourselves to standing. I shoved my body hard against his and kissed him full on the mouth with all the awful unspoken love I had for him.

"I gotta go t'work." Reluctantly, I let the demands of a day already begun seep into my consciousness. "I gotta go . . ." I mumbled. "I'm gonna be late . . ." And I kissed his eyelids, his freckled cheeks, his crooked crook-nose. We pulled apart with milky strands of cum at ass and cock. The last tenuous threads to connect us.

Out in the hall, in my shorts and work boots, I said, "Will ya stay awhile . . . a few days . . . a week or so, maybe? Will ya?"

He stood in the doorway, his man's body filling the space, and gave me his little-boy-lost, sad-eyed smile. He smiled, but didn't answer—not yes, not no. He said nothing at all as if all his thoughts had gone elsewhere, gone deep inside him to a place safe from indifference, cruelty and pain.

In the street outside, I turned and looked up at my window. He was standing there, standing straight and stiff and awkward, like he knew he didn't belong. He waved but his smile was gone. I would've called to him, yelled goodbye or something, but I couldn't make a sound. It was as if someone behind me had his arms around my chest and was squeezing with all the strength in his body.

The Boy Who Never Told

DAVY WAS COMING BACK HOME for a while because Dad had cancer. Dad and I were sitting in the kitchen when we heard big-booted thudding on the front veranda. I watched Dad's smile of recognition distort into a grimace as he pushed himself away from the table and rose to his feet, carefully, painfully.

"It's him," he said to me over his shoulder, and he shuffled down the hall.

"It's me, Dad." It must have been Davy's voice, but it was not a voice I would have recognized. Apprehension clutched my stomach.

"Christ, Dave, I wouldn't have known you," Dad was saying, unlatching the screen door. "You've put some meat on. And you're the color of a flamin' Abo."

I heard Davy's dry, raspy laugh and the screen door's metal hinges squealing. The door slammed shut behind them and his voice was inside the hall. "How ya feelin', Dad?"

I felt suddenly chilled in the warm kitchen. My heart was hammering and my hands were clammy. Dad followed Davy into the kitchen, and I stood abruptly and backed away from the table and rubbed my hands together. They slid against their own moisture. Across the room, Davy was smiling, looking directly into my eyes. His deep dark eyes were glittering, eyes I had not seen in five years but had never forgotten. The sight of them again made my breath catch.

"G'day, Phil," he said. Coal black unkempt curls seemed to tumble, willy-nilly, about his face, over his ears, across his broad forehead, over his upturned collar. His damp shirt was split open to his waist, exposing a deeply bronzed expanse of muscled chest and abdomen. The blatant masculine virility he exuded unnerved me and I lowered my eyes to the thick column of his neck where drops of moisture clung to the smooth tanned skin.

"G'day, Davy," I said. And I looked away. I felt my own sweat trickling under my armpits like captured crawling flies.

* * *

I WAS SIX YEARS OLD when Mum sat me down on her lap and explained to me in a serious voice that we were going to move to another place, live in a house with rooms upstairs and a yard in the back where I could play. There would be a daddy there for me, which I had never had, and a big brother too, and we would all live together as a loving family. Oddly enough I cannot recall the early stages of our life together. Those first years occupy my memory as a continuous shadowy blur, a time I suffered through with a shyness so fierce that it was a kind of pain.

I shared a room with my new half-brother, occupied a bed in that room, was given a desk and a chair and a small chest of drawers of my own, but in his eyes I was not there at all. He was twelve, twice my age and already showing signs of burgeoning manhood, when I was thrust into his singular world. He ignored me totally and I melted into non-existence, into utter indifference, into living oblivion. Yet I observed his life in minute detail, unnoticed, like an unseen insect on the wall. I watched him with a restless melancholy, a yearning need for some simple recognition, some small acknowledgement of my puny existence. I watched him in silence for if I spoke his frown would deepen and his eyes would narrow as though the very sound of my voice was intolerable to him.

Every morning, lying still and silent in my bed, prickly sensations passing through me, I watched him slip naked from his bed, his lithe new muscles tanned and glowing, his shoulders square and broad, his curving buttocks plump and pristine white. I watched in avid fascination as his dangling cock slapped against his downy thighs. Its color and shape reminded me of a bloated oversized grub clad in an almost luminous silken skin. Sometimes, when he flung back the sheet, it was fully erect and bounced up and down, stiffly, and thumped heavily against his flat belly as if it had a life of its own. I longed to touch it, to stroke the pert pale-pink mushroom head where centered was a single moist red eye.

Every morning, I watched him dress, his unaware body oozing casual strength and grace. He wore faded denim jeans and tee-shirts or short-sleeved shirts with the sleeves rolled up to his shoulders. He turned up his collars and pulled out his shirttails. Scuffed tennis shoes were worn with mismatched laces and without socks. His dark curls were greased to shiny black and combed ripplingly back on both sides of his head so that they met precisely at the back in a vertical line. In front, over his forehead, his hair fell in a tapering vee. Standing wide-legged in front of the mirror, he would comb both sides of the vee carefully upward, following each sweep of the comb with a smoothing hand. Looking at himself with unguarded admiration, he would hold the comb horizontally over his head and with a quick deft flick he would send the point of the vee toppling over his forehead in perfectly placed disorder. Often, as I watched, his eyes in the mirror caught me staring. I would instantly turn away, but not before he had flung me a look of burning hatred.

* * *

"HERE'S DAVE," Dad announced proudly as he followed his son into the kitchen. "We haven't seen the young bugger for five flamin' years. Looks fit as a fiddle, don't he?"

I nodded. The brief glimpse I had of Davy in the kitchen doorway before I looked away told me that he was, though now a man, just as unbearably handsome as he had been as a boy. I wanted to look at him, but I could not bring my eyes back to his face, his eyes.

"Phil talks about you all the time," Dad was saying to Davy. My face flushed. "Them snaps you sent two Christmases ago, he's got stuck up over his bed. The one of you coming out of the creek, in your flamin' birthday suit, seems to be his favorite."

I was blushing violently. I could feel Davy's eyes burning into me. I heard his deep-throated chuckle. Knowing I had to escape, I looked around the room wildly, like a caged animal. "I gotta . . . I gotta go to work," I mumbled, stumbling over a chair, edging around the table to the door. With eyes averted I brushed past Davy. I felt the warmth radiating from his body. The smell of him, his fresh sweat smell, was intense and alarmingly familiar.

"You're lookin' pretty fit yourself, Phil " he said, softly, as our shoulders touched. Then as I moved down the hall to the stairs I heard him say to Dad, "He's growed up to be a real good-looking kid."

"Yeah. It's hard to believe he was such as scrawny little bugger."

"His hair suits him long like that. I bet he's got more sheilas than ya can shake a stick at."

"Nah. He don't have no girlfriends—no friends at all, that I know of. He was always the shy one . . ."

Upstairs, in my room, I stretched out on my bed. It was too early to go to work. I rolled onto my left side and looked across to his bed, the empty unmade bed that I had looked at for five years. Five years of erupting into sudden angers, collapsing into deep desolations, sleeping after anguished sobbings. Looking now, but trying not to remember, not even to think, I turned away to face the wall. His recent gaze and recent words were about my body like intimate caresses, and while I fought not to remember, I remembered in sudden vividness everything I had struggled to forget. As I so often did, I remembered that day five years ago when Davy left. I could see our room as if I was pressed flat as paint on the ceiling, a third person with camera-lens eyes, looking down. And looking down I saw

Two boys in a room on a warm summer evening. The younger boy, Phillip, is sitting at a desk before an open notebook which is bluish white in the faintly tremulous glare of the fluorescent desk lamp. Through the dark screen comes a sweet moist smell of fresh-cut grass and more pungent odors of lilac and petrol. Phillip tips his chair back from the harshly lit desk where he is writing. He pauses for a moment, chewing the scarred end of a ballpoint pen, and says to his brother:

"How d'ya spell accommodate?"

"Dunno," the other boy says, after a deliberate silence.

"I know it's got two cees but I'm not sure if there's one or two ems."

After another silence, "Who gives a flyin' fuck."

"Just thought you might know." There is a hint of sarcasm in the reply.

"Then ya fuckin' thought wrong." David, dark-haired with sleepy brown eyes, a ruggedly handsome, moody seventeen-year-old, is lying bored on his bed with bare feet slapped up against the sailing-boat print wallpaper. A car door slams. The light from the desk lamp trembles faintly but perceptibly. The boys' parents are going out for the evening to play the poker machines at the RSL *Club. A motor sounds, and becomes softer and softer and disappears.*

"Two ems don't look right," Phillip says, frowning in annoyance, crossing his arms over his pale bony chest. Then, glowering down at his brother, angered by his indifference, his indolence, he says, "Get your damned feet off the wall, why don't you."

"Fuck off, scarecrow. Me feet's clean." David has just showered and is naked except for a soggy towel wrapped loosely around his waist. His curly hair is sleeked back, still glistening wet and dripping on the bedclothes.

The younger boy glares and sucks air through his front teeth. "Fuck off yourself, shitface," he says, under his breath. Tipping his chair forward, he returns to his homework, writing painstakingly with the ballpoint pen on the lined notepaper. Phillip has sandy blond hair and blue-green eyes that turn downward at the corners and a full red mouth. He is more willowy than skinny, fine-featured and flat-muscled, unlike his brother in every way.

"Two cees and one em is what it is," Phillip says with feigned confidence, cocking his head to get another point of view of what he has written. He turned eleven six months ago and has grown suddenly tall, almost as tall as his brother who is prob-

ably short for his age. Some catch-up fleshing out will eventually improve his physique, but meanwhile he is not at all gangling or awkward, possessing rather a lithe-limbed, elongated elegance. But this is not how Phillip sees himself. Alongside his brother he feels freakishly tall, painfully thin, narrow of shoulder and hip, with slender wrists and ankles, altogether too fine-boned to be a boy. And David continually reminds him of their differences, calling him "scarecrow," jeering at his girl's delicate skin and long lashes, mocking his gentle self-effacing manner and diligence.

"What didja say?" David is suddenly sitting up, scowling.

"Accommodate's got two cees and one em."

"Before that. Ya said somethin' before that."

"No. I didn't." The boy lies because he is frightened.

"Ya called me a fuckin' name."

"I didn't," Phillip lies. The untruth and the fear show in his timid, sloping eyes.

"I'll teach ya t'call me fuckin' names, ya friggin' little fairy." David lunges forward and grabs his brother's wrist. The pen rips across the notebook and clatters to the floor.

"I didn't, Davy. Honest." Phillip struggles to release his arm but the older boy is so much stronger.

"I'll fuckin' teach ya . . ." As David grapples with the frightened boy, dragging him onto the bed, the towel drops away from his waist. His exposed swinging cock is already engorged.

"No, Davy. Please. You're hurting me."

"I'll hurt ya a helluva lot more if ya don't keep still and shut yer face."

"Please, Davy . . ." Phillip continues to struggle. "Davy, please . . ."

David hits the boy across the mouth with the back of his hand. There is a sharp cracking sound and blood trickles freely from the gash on Phillip's lip. He is still now, and quiet, except for his whimpering.

"Stop sniveling, ya little sissy, or ya'll cop another one." David flips the boy onto his stomach and climbs on the bed, kneeling between the long slender legs. Phillip chokes himself into silence and stares in terror over his shoulder as he feels

inertia, a wearying of muscles, a dolor of the blood. He is so very tired. He longs to lie this way drowsily forever. His eyes are closed and he hopes he will never have to open them, and he savors the completeness of his exhausted body, sinking into oblivion, drifting away into infinity, swallowed up by redeeming sleep. He is so very very tired.

* * *

HOT SLIVERS of late afternoon sunlight soaked through the slatted blind. I opened my eyes and the room was dim. Faintly, I heard voices coming up from the kitchen. Davy *was* here. My remembering was not a dream, had never been a dream. I undressed quickly, changing into my work clothes, and tiptoed down the unswept stairs. I advanced cautiously down the hall and paused near the open kitchen door, sucking in my stomach to seal my breath.

"...and he never finished school," Dad was saying, "After you left he wasn't the same. Seemed to lose interest in everything."

I heard the sigh of bottles on the plastic tablecloth. They were drinking beer, smoking, talking about me.

"What's he doin' now, then? His job?" Davy asked.

"He works nights at the factory is all I know. He never ses what he actually does there. He never ses anything much."

"Was he pretty upset when Mum died?"

"Yeah, for a while. But she was bad for months before she went. I had the feeling he was more upset coz you never came back for the funeral."

"She was *his* mother, fer crissakes, not mine," Davy said, defensively. Then, after a long pause, "I thought I'd only be in the way. I thought he'd resent me bein' around."

"Bugger it, Dave, the kid worshipped you."

"Nah, he couldn't of. I was always such a mean bastard to 'im."

"He did, Dave, he did. Christ, he still does."

"Nah, I don't think so..."

I moved away from the kitchen door, sliding a foot backwards, bringing the other foot back silently beside it, retreating this way down the hall until I reached the screen door. I lifted the latch and bit my lip against the squeal of the hinges. I heard Dad's faltering voice ask the question I had asked myself a thousand times:

"Why, Dave... why didja leave like that? So sudden. Without a word, or anything."

I waited for Davy's reply, but as I knew there would be none I stepped carefully across the veranda's dry-rotted boards and down the rickety steps to the concrete path. I made my way, breathing again, through the unkempt yard to the darkening street.

As I walked to the factory I thought about that night, the night he left home. And the endless nights that followed, and the weeks, the months, the years after. Summer upon summer overlapped in accumulating layers of sameness and boredom and lethargy. At school I did poorly in everything. I became silent and sullen. My worsening achievements and withdrawn behavior were tolerated by my teachers. Among my schoolmates I made no enemies, no friends. School oppressed me; the dreary cream and green tiled corridors, the forbidding rows of battered lockers, the grime-encrusted windowsills, and the graffitied walls. Often I was sick and stayed home, listlessly reading and daydreaming. Reading less and less, daydreaming more and more.

At home, I lay for hours in my gloomy room, blind drawn, hands behind my head, looking up at the shadowed ceiling. Watching and waiting, empty and exhausted. And sometimes, as I lay there, I let myself be filled with a fearful dreamy exhilaration. Closing my eyes, I would raise my hand to my face, imagining someone else's hand. I would press the palm softly to my cheek, imagining someone else's caressing touch. I would move my hand between my legs to feel myself go hard in someone else's hand. Then, stroking my cock with a fierce sensual excitement, I would shudder in an ecstasy of desolation. I wiped the stickiness from my stomach with disappointment and frustration, and seized by a feverish sorrow, my heart beating painfully, I would bring my hand to my forehead to feel the sickly heat of my brow.

As the summers dragged on, and despite my indifference to the changes in my body, I grew bigger and stronger and more potent. But it seemed as if the older I got the more there was nothing to do. I longed for something, anything to do, but at the same time I did not want to do anything. I longed to be left alone, and yet I could not endure my insufferable loneliness. I longed to be free of my body which seemed to be the source of only disquieting sensations and misplaced desires. And yet a sweet yearning restlessness gnawed at my soul. I had the not unpleasant sense that I was waiting. Waiting, expectantly. But waiting for what? Waiting for my own share of time? Time will cast its own judgment, I thought. Time unites, separates, reunites. Or does it?

I trudged on, heavy of heart and foot, and it was dark when I passed through the high wire-netting factory gates.

* * *

IT WAS STILL DARK when I returned home, though the new day was beginning to lighten the horizon. It was not dark in my room—*our* room again—because Davy had left a small lamp burning. The same small lamp he would not leave on at night when I was little and terrified of the dark and begged, pleaded for it to be left on. Davy was in his bed, facing the wall. I turned off the light and undressed, fumbling, in the darkness. Sitting gingerly on my bed, I drew up my knees, hugging them to me for comfort, to assuage a sudden sadness. In his presence, as before, I felt inadequate, unappealing, a pale naked serious youth, with slender hands, untidy straw-colored hair, and a frown of stern concentration. And for a long while I sat like that, nervously listening for something other than his breathing. Faint watery plumbing noises were audible from the bathroom. Nothing else, just muted gurglings and his measured breath.

The dark walls, the dark ceiling, the dark quiet of his slumbering began to press on me from all sides in a gentle conspiracy. Even in the dark, in the familiar, almost intense silence of our shared room, I could tell he was not asleep. I slowly raised my head from my knees and turned to face him. I felt a sudden ache of longing, and with a throb of expectation I mouthed his name.

"Davy..."

In the silence I saw that the sky outside was now dully luminous. Silver gray.

"Phil?" I shuddered when I heard his voice, my name. Bedsprings creaked as he rolled over, repositioning his body to see me hunched and silhouetted against the first morning light.

"Phil?" he said again, softly, tentatively, and with that alone I knew he had been crying.

"Yeah," I whispered.

"Ya never told them. Didja?"

"No,"

"Ya never told them about what I done t'ya?"

"No."

"Why, why not?"

"I...I don't know." I did know why, but I did not know how to say it; that I had not felt violated by him that night, but wanted, needed by him for the first time in my life. I turned my head to the window. Through the tilted slats of the blind, through the transparent ghost of my face reflected in the smudged glass, I could see the dawn sky brightening. When I turned my head away from the window enough pale light now filtered into the room to illuminate the pain in Davy's dark wet eyes.

"I'm sorry," he said, "I'm sorry for what I done."

"I know," I whispered.

"It's why I left. Why I never came back."

"I know."

"I wanted to come back. I couldn't...because..."

"It doesn't matter."

"Christ, Phil, it matters. It has to matter. You must hate my guts."

"No," I whispered, "I don't." I was on the verge of tears. I pressed my forehead to my knees and fought them back. "I always thought you hated *me*," I said.

"Yeah, at first. I guess I did. I never wanted no brother.

I was jealous of ya. Christ, Phil, I was such an ignorant bastard."

"I wanted so . . . so much for you to like me." My voice was broken by a sob. I had lost the battle with my tears.

"Christ, Phil, don't . . ."

"I'm okay," I said, but I couldn't stop myself from crying.

"Phil, don't . . ." He was there on my bed, his arm across my sagging shoulders, wrapping me, folding me into his body. His naked heat and strength flowed into me. My head was pounding and my heart was pounding, my brain was bursting and tears fell from my eyes and ran warmly down the insides of my thighs.

"I'm okay," I gasped between convulsing sobs.

He lifted my face and touched me and wet his fingertips with my tears and said my name. When I opened my eyes to him, my sobs subsiding, there was something in the way he was looking at me, the way his dark eyes burned through to the core of me, that caused me to let the breathless words tumble out. "I love you." And before I could draw another breath his mouth was on my face, my eyes, my wet cheeks, on my mouth.

"Oh Jesus, Phil . . ." His parted lips closed over mine, and he pushed me back gently on the bed, stretching his body across me. His kisses were feverish, passionate, and I felt the throbbing heat of his hard cock press into my belly. I wrapped my arms around his powerful back and thrust my body against his in frantic need.

"Oh Phil, Phil . . . I want you so bad," he moaned, kissing me as if his mouth would devour me. A choking cry caught in his throat, his body shuddered, and his cock jerked violently on my belly. Thick spurting cum was hot on my flesh from my navel to my neck.

His orgasm subsided but he did not stop kissing me, and his cock seemed even more urgently erect. His suctioning lips and darting tongue traveled each fleshy contour of my torso, inflaming me. I writhed and squirmed and undulated in his caressing hands. Suddenly, I felt my cock consumed by his mouth, almost brutally. My hands gripped his head, fingers plunging into the thick mass of curls. I could hear myself gasping for air, grunting in an agony of intense pleasure. For a fleeting moment, before the bliss that was rising in me like warm mercury rose faster and faster and bubbled over, I was aware of a small flicker of sunlight glinting through blind. With my dazzled eyes clenched shut against that pencil thickness of unforgiving light, with my heart galloping and my fingers clutching in the roots of his hair, I jerked my hips up from the bed with a single involuntary cry to drive my erupting cock deeply into his throat.

When I was spent and still and sun-dappled he moved to kiss me again.

"It's always been you I wanted. No one else," he said, speaking with his moist lips brushing my mouth. A warm rush of saliva and semen flowed across my lips, across my tongue. I savored and swallowed and smiled gratefully. He licked my lips and kissed me deeply. The mass of his body pinned me to the mattress, but I seemed weightless, vaporous beneath him as if an enormous load had been lifted from me; the burden of my years of crushing loneliness.

"When ya first came, I couldn't stand the sight of ya. I never wanted to share me room. I told Dad he'd have t'kill me first, an' he bloody near did. Jesus, I hated ya before I ever even *seen* ya," Davy said, huskily, his mouth nuzzling my ear. "As we grew, got older, I started t'get these strange feelings. Weird feelings I didn't understand, that really scared me. The things me mates at school talked about doing with girls, I wanted to do with you." He raised his hips slightly and lowered them again to connect, to voluptuously slide the broad underbelly of his cock full-length on mine. "It's always been you I wanted. Always you."

"But you left," I said, stroking the damp curls back from his temple.

"I had to. After that night, after it happened. What I did... it was all wrong... I hit ya... I hurt ya... when what I really wanted was..." His voice faded away and his head dropped into the curve of my shoulder.

"When I woke up you were gone," I told him. "I wanted to tell you it was all right. That it wasn't wrong."

"I had to go. There wasn't nothing else I could do."

"When I woke you'd gone, and there was blood on the sheets and on the pillow. I put my hand between my legs and it was sticky with blood and cum. My blood and your cum, mixed together. And that didn't seem wrong because I... I loved you."

"Phil, Jesus. I never knew,"

"I wanted to tell you. But you'd gone."

"Phil, Jesus..."

"It's all right. I love you, Davy. I loved you then, and I love you still."

"Oh, Phil..."

"Do it to me, Davy, Do it to me now, like you wanted to then. I want you to, Davy."

"Oh, Phil, I want ya so bad. Yer all I ever wanted."

"Do it, Davy. Do it to me."

I pushed his shoulders gently and he slid down my body, trailing kisses, sinking down on his knees between my legs. I opened to him, raising my knees and spreading my thighs, tilting my pelvis to him in invitation. He bent forward and dipped his head between my open legs. There was sudden wet heat on the tender membranes of my exposed asshole. His tongue was pressing there, then lapping and lathering, then pressing deeper, darting. I sucked in air; an obscene hissing of pleasure through my teeth. His tongue delved and probed snakelike in my anus.

Davy lifted his head, sitting slightly bent forward to watch himself insert a finger into my pink supple-lipped slit. He watched his deft manipulation with his mouth half open, his eyes half closed, his face expressing a concentration so rapt it resembled a trance. His beautiful bronzed body, shimmering in the striations of sunlight cast through the blind, was poised over me in rutting animal alertness, his cock jutting rigidly out from between thick thighs, engorged and ominously drooling. The finger drew out slowly to its tip, and plunged, and again I sucked in hissing air.

When he knew I was ready, when he felt the ring of muscle stretched and relaxed and ready, he grasped the base of his cock and guided its broad glistening head to my saliva-oozing hole. The touch was fleshy warm and firm, determined and gently insistent. I gripped my buttocks, craving fulfillment, and pulled my asslips open into a surprised little circle to cap his cock's blunt head. As he bore down for entry, the sensation at first was thrilling, but as the pressure relentlessly increased so did a gradual throbbing discomfort. There was a stab of pain, then another, and another, and at the point where the pain might have become unbearable there was a rushing, swelling sensation of fullness, a sudden pleasurable sense of completeness. I knew then that he was inside me.

"Jesus, Phil . . . that's so good," he sighed, pushing into me, smothering my face and neck with open-mouthed kisses.

"It's good for me, Davy. Good for me, too," I told him, but there were no words to tell him how it really felt. I slid my fingers to my ass to fondle the sleek shaft as it slowly sank further into me. When there was nothing left of his cock to hold, I held his balls, cupping them, amazed by their pendular weight and hugeness. Then I relaxed my body and yielded to him.

"Fuck me, Davy . . . Fuck me . . . fuck me," I whispered, and I gave myself joyfully to him for the consummation of our long-held love.

"Oh, Phil, fuckin' Jesus . . ." he gasped. "Oh, Phil, my lovely Phil . . ." His mouth and hands and cock all seemed to be fucking me. I was dreamily aware of soft cloying anatomy joining and parting, of bodies rocking gently to and fro, of muscles flexing and rippling, sinews tensing and tautening.

The flesh of his body enveloped me, penetrated deeply within me, became a pulsing living part of me. I felt my stomach and groin and thighs flowing into his. I felt my arms flowing within his arms until my fingers slipped within his fingers. I felt my toes wriggling within his toes, my shoulders moving to become part of him, my mouth melting into his mouth. My breathing flowed to become his breathing and my cock was his cock. I felt my heart flowing within his heart until they pounded as one.

Our coupling consumed us totally, overwhelmed us, and we called out each other's names in soaring rapture and revelation. And when at last we fell back to earth, drained, exhausted, our bodies locked and sweated together, we closed our eyes and slept a sun-warmed sleep in the bright morning light.

It was four hours later when I woke up. Looking down from the ceiling with my bird's-eye view I saw

Two young men in a room on a warm summer morning. The two beds on opposite walls are unmade. One is empty and on the other David and Phillip are sprawled naked, arms and legs tangled, sheets gathered and wrapped and pulled away from the corners of the mattress. Phillip, the younger of the two men, still not much more than a boy, yawns and carefully frees his right arm from beneath David's body. He stretches it up into the dusty sunlight and shakes it to regain circulation.

From the kitchen below can be heard the hacking cough of a sick man who takes comfort in knowing his sons are upstairs. David's head rolls to one side, but he does not wake. Phillip gazes into the face that is so close he sees only segments: the shadow of dark stubble over the top lip and under the upsweep of cheekbone, the sheen of perspiration across the weather-lined forehead, a bubble of spit at the corner of the mouth that expands and contracts with each long breath.

Phillip lifts his head slightly, enough to kiss the brown nipple nearby, then lowers it again, his eyes half-closing drowsily. There is a smile on his lips. He is smiling because today David will have no need to leave home as he did once before. And never will again. He is smiling because today he has no need to be sad or serious or lonely. And never will again.

Looking down, that is how I saw myself; smiling like the happy child I should have been but never was.

Hot for the Treatment

IT WAS SUNDAY MORNING, the twenty-sixth of February, one week and two days after my seventeenth birthday, when I found the wart on my cock. I made this discovery at exactly eight minutes after eight. The time is indelibly imprinted on my mind because of a numerical coincidence. I was measuring my erection (I measured my erection *religiously* every Sunday morning—the length first then the circumference—with a tape measure borrowed from Mum's sewing basket the previous evening and secreted away in my pillow case), when I happened to glance at the clock on my bedside table, seeing with amusement that both the hours and the minutes agreed with the number of inches it took the tape to reach from the base of my cock to the tip. Everything was reading eight. My smug self-satisfied grin, however, did not last eight seconds as the tape slackened and fell away, revealing the wart.

"Bloody hell!" I said aloud. scrambling off the bed, hopping to the bookshelves with my pajama pants around my ankles. I knew vaguely about warts; a kid in primary school had shown me the one he had on his left hand, but as he wasn't a friend or even in my class I hadn't paid much attention. I pulled down *The Concise Oxford Dictionary of Current English* and began thumbing furiously, finding the double-u's, flipping pages, scanning the columns, reading the words silently with my lips: *warrant, warranty, warren, warrior, wart . . .*

"Wart! Bloody hell!" I gasped. Hearing it was like a stab wound. I wasn't breathing as I read:

wart (wart), n. Small hardish excrescence on skin caused by abnormal growth of papillae, . . . "What are they, for fuck's sake?" I said.

...similar lump on stem etc. of plant...

"I'm not a plant. Why do I have a lump on *my* stem?" Now I was flipping the pages backwards to the p's to find out what was growing abnormally. My finger slid down the column, the words emerging from under my nail: *papaw, paper, papier mâché, papilionaceous, papilla...* "There it is. Thank God!"

papilla, n. (pl. -ae). Small nipple-like protuberance in part or organ of the body; (bot.) small fleshy projection on plant...

"Fuck the plants," I said, and begin piecing together the information: "A wart is a small hardish excrescence on the skin caused by abnormal growth of (papillae) small nipple-like protuberances in a part or organ of the body." It made no sense. As usual, the dictionary offered nothing more than contradictions and redundancies, a gabble of meaningless words.

Kicking off my pajama pants, I slumped back dejectedly on the bed, momentarily defeated by the vagaries of the English language. Then, suddenly inspired by a fresh possibility, I spread my legs and raised my dispirited cock with a tentative thumb and forefinger, for surely at that early hour I'd simply imagined the wart. It was a trick of morning light, a stray bit of lint. I looked, and it wasn't. Close inspection confirmed a risen lump of three-dimensional flesh. An excrescence. Its grotesque and ominous reality filled me with revulsion. I fought back an all-pervading sense of doom and the bitter taste of despair soured my mouth. A faint, almost unfelt flame began to lick along my marrow, the up-until-now unthought-of prospect of death. Would this insidious attachment continue to grow and, cancer-like, gradually, agonizingly devour my body? Was its obscene presence a warrant for my untimely demise?

I desperately needed answers. Throwing on a bathrobe, I crept hurriedly from my room and tiptoed swiftly down the hall to my dad's den. The *Encyclopædia Britannica* formed a monumental bank of stern and imposing tomes on the bottom shelf of the wall-to-wall mahogany bookcase. Consulting the index, I split open the musty pages of the appropriate volume that creaked with disuse. I located at last and read:

WART, *or* VERRUCA, *a well-defined small growth of varying shape on the skin surface, caused by a virus.* "Bloody hell!" I gasped aloud. "A germ!" *They may occur as isolated lesions or grow profusely, especially in moist regions of the body surface.* "Grow profusely!" I felt my crotch. It was moist. *The methods of treatment are numerous, generally aimed at disintegrating the wart with minimum of scarring.* "Jesus! I'm going to be scarred!" *. . . using electric or chemical means or freezing.* "Jesus! Electric shocks! My dick frozen!" *Warts, contrary to popular superstition, are not contracted from the skin or excretions of the toad.*

The toad was the last straw. I barely made it to the bathroom in time before I vomited. Seated on the lavatory, my evacuated stomach clutched, my face cooling in a dampened towel, I struggled to get my thoughts in order. If I went back to bed, I conjectured, I might fall asleep, then wake up again properly to find this was all a horrible nightmare. But when I looked down at my cock drooping despondently in the bowl, I caught a shadowed glimpse of the "well-defined small growth." It was only too real. This is the blackest day in my life, I thought, and in so thinking *Black's Medical Dictionary* materialized in my mind.

Black's Medical Dictionary was not kept in my dad's den but in the company of cookbooks in the kitchen. Revived by the possibility of enlightenment and salvation, I made my way quietly and somewhat unsteadily to Mum's domain. The book was heaven-sent. Its friendly well-fingered leaves parted immediately and miraculously to reval an entire page of plain down-to-earth English devoted to the subject in question.

WARTS, *or* VERRUCAE, *are small, solid growths, arising from the surface of the skin. They are due to a papavavirus infection of the skin. They are highly infectious, and it is estimated that ten per cent of the population suffer from them. The infection is most likely to be spread in schools by hand-holding games, and among adolescents by walking barefoot on gymnasium floors and in swimming baths.* COMMON WARTS *develop on the skin of children and young persons on the knuckles, on the backs of the hands, and on the knees. Occasionally such warts come out in a crop.* TREATMENT. *There is much to be said for the old advice that the best way to manage warts is to let them manage themselves. Quite often they disappear spontaneously...*

I read no further. This was what I needed to know; leave it alone and the wart, in its own good time, would go away by itself. I was elated. I scampered back to my bedroom and flinging aside my robe, sprawling on the bed, I rewarded myself and my soon-to-be-well cock with a slow sensuous and patronizingly generous jacking off. Dabbling my fingers absently in the cooling puddles of cum on my chest and belly, I slipped into a contented half-sleep, comforted by the learned words recently read and assured once again that—for the eradication of warts, at least—the pen was mightier than the sword.

A daily check revealed no change in the size and disposition of the wart. There were no outwardly visible indications of its impending disappearance. By the end of the week, if anything, it looked larger, more virulent.

"I'm a goner," I thought.

"Relax," I told myself. "It's a temporary condition." But somewhere deep inside, in my heart of hearts, there lurked an unpleasant queasiness. I was not reassured. Something had to be done. I tried cold showers, prolonged soaks in hot baths, applications of tincture of iodine, antiseptic sponges. I found a medicated ointment in the bathroom cabinet which I applied in liberal quantities every morning for a week. My cock tingled and stayed painfully erect until lunchtime each day, and my underpants showed blotchy stains of such a sickly sulphurous yellow that I feared Mum would suspect me of incontinence. For all of this, the wart remained. Impervious. Invincible.

"Who can I turn to?" I asked myself.

"My parents," I answered, without any real conviction, as I joined them at the breakfast table.

"Good morning, Bunny Rabbit," Mum said with suffocating sweetness as I sat. She kissed the top of my head, fingered my ear lobes, and lifted the silver cover from the steaming plate before me. Dad, who was completely hidden by the Sunday *Sun-Herald,* made no acknowledgment of my arrival. Breakfast with my parents had never been the high point of my day, but with the arrival of the wart it was now an ordeal I could scarcely suffer through. The sausages looked warty and the poached eggs seemed infected. I couldn't drink the orange juice without feeling little lumps sliding down my throat.

"Guess what?" I announced, bright and breezy, to introduce the topic of warts into the as yet non-existent meal-table conversation. "I saw this chap with these incredible bumps all over his hands. Um, he was driving the school bus."

Dad continued to ignore me but Mum smiled indulgently. "You don't go to school in the school bus, dear. I drive you in the Daimler."

"Oh, yeah... that's right. It wasn't the school bus." My nervous laughter barely concealed the deceit in my voice. "Ha. Ha. It was a... um, just a *bus* bus."

"I do wish you wouldn't use public transportation, dear. It's not sanitary, and the people who use it... well, poor things, they *have* to use it."

"I like buses," I said, defensively, detesting the meekness in my voice, knowing I had lost control of the conversation. If I'd ever had any.

"You know, dear, I'm only too happy to take you wherever you need to go. And if it's not far you have a lovely new bicycle to ride."

"I know, but..." I was effectively silenced, my feebly attempted dissidence smothered under a mountain of motherlove. The pursuit of any less-than-superficial communication was, as always, sidetracked by Mum's misguided sense of maternal purpose. And as always, I was left feeling frustrated and angry. More angry with myself for not hating nearly as much as I thought I should the daily chauffering to school, and the "lovely new bicycle" that was given to me whenever the current one's shiny brightness dulled. Fortunately we lived within walking distance of the beach and my best friend Smudge. Smudge! Why hadn't I thought of him before? Of course, I could tell Smudge. He, of all people, would be sympathetic to my predicament.

We finished breakfast in silence—they eating, me shoveling bacon-and-egg parts to the center of the plate to compact them into one single (wart-shaped) hillock. Excusing myself with the grace and charm expected of me—a grimace and a couple of grunts—I dashed to my room to telephone my best friend. His mum answered the phone on the seventh ring. She sounded asleep.

"Good morning, Mrs. Lawson. May I speak to Arnold, please?" I said cheerfully, in my best speaking-to-parents mode, remembering even to substitute "can" with "may."

"Certainly you are able to, young man, but the question to which you seek an answer is will you be permitted to." That was not what Smudge's mum said, that was what Miss Prowse, our English teacher, said about the use of "can" and "may." Smudge's mum said:

"Jesus friggin' Christ, it's twelve friggin' minutes past nine on a friggin' Sunday morning. Youse bloody kids'll be the death of me. Piss the fuck off, willya." Clunk. And hung up.

Smudge and I were in the same class at school and had been best friends, virtually inseparable, since our first year in high school. As there was nothing about him of which my parents would have approved; his appearance, his manners, his clothes, his parents' house, and especially his parents, I had kept his existence a closely guarded secret. Our out-of-school activities were clandestine, cat-and-mouse affairs, and the well-planned devious manner in which they were conducted only served to tighten the bonds of our friendship, making it more intense, more illicitly exciting.

How and why Smudge and I fell into our unshakable, impenetrable friendship is one of life's many minor perversities. We were total opposites in every respect. He was a living example of everything my parents had conditioned me not to be. He wasn't even good-looking. I don't mean to imply that he was a sight for sore eyes, but he wasn't exactly knock-you-down-dead handsome either. I mean when you saw him parading on the beach in his Speedos or biking down the street in just his Stubbies, Michelangelo's David or Praxiteles' Hermes didn't come to mind. Comparatively speaking, if my looks could be considered average—which is certainly not what my mum considered them to be—then Smudge could only be described as being exceptionally average. I guess that's why I liked him.

At eleven-thirty, with once-bitten-twice-shy fingers on the dial, I again rotated out the Lawsons' telephone number. And held my breath. I listened to three interminable rings, getting purple in the face, and then there was a lick and Smudge's nasal drawl:

"Lawson's loony bin."

"G'day, mate," I said, breathing a huge sigh of relief.

"G'day yerself, ya drongo."

"How's things?"

"Fuckin' marvelous, mate. How's yerself?"

Smudge's outlook on life was simple-minded, straightforward and sun-drenched. I felt better already. "Good," I answered, then remembering why I was calling. "Well, actually I've got a bit of problem."

"What's up?"

"Um... well... what would you do if you woke up one morning and found a wart on your thingee?"

There was a long silence followed by a short laugh.

"Jees, mate. I'd cut it off and feed it to the doggee."

"We don't have a dog."

"Ya don't 'ave no wart on yer dick, neither, ya ratbag."

"Yeah..." A pause. "I do."

"Garn, don't gimme the raw prawn."

"It's true. Honest."

"Holy shit!"

I could hear him breathing through another long silence. No laughter followed, just his crackly sing-song voice. "Jees, I dunno what to say, mate. I mean... like, does it hurt or anything?"

"No, but..." My words thickened. I felt them lump in my throat.

"Jees, mate. I'm real sorry. I mean ... like, *real* sorry ..." His voice trailed away, as thick suddenly as mine.

"Can you come over?"

"Yeah, course. But what about them?"

"Wait a while. Twenty minutes. They're leaving to play golf."

"Right-o." A pause. "... and, hey, buggerlugs ..."

"What?"

"No worries. Okay?"

"Who's worried?" I tried to make my reply seem confidently nonchalant, but I think he'd already hung up before I said it. I wasn't at all hopeful that Smudge would have any practical suggestions but I felt some comfort knowing that I could rely on his one-hundred-per-cent sympathy.

Smudge's bike came to a clattering halt on the brick walk outside my window at almost the same instant his head appeared over the sill. His sun-bleached dirty-blond hair was sticking out in all directions and his face was flushed and most with sweat. He dove, head first, as if propelled by some ingenious exterior spring, and with a nimble shoulder roll arrived in the center of the room on his feet, hands on hips, perfectly balanced. This was his customary method of entry, but today it was not enhanced by his lopsided look-at-me smile. He was barefoot, wearing patched hand-me-down jeans and a battered grease-stained shirt with one sleeve rolled up to the elbow, the other hanging loosely, unbuttoned, at his wrist.

"G'day," I said, managing a weak smile.

He stood there, taking deep breaths, looking at me as if I'd recently arrived from outer space. Which is a bit how I felt anyway.

"Jees, mate," he said, finally.

I tried to improve on my half-hearted attempt at a smile and I gave a little wave of my hand without raising my arm, which seemed to be a particularly stupid thing to do.

"Jees, mate," was all he kept saying, over and over like a cracked gramophone record. He was beginning to make me feel I had ten minutes to live.

"It's not *that* bad. I mean, I'm not going to *die* or anything," I said. But there was death in my heart.

"Jees, mate."

"The books all say it's a temporary condition. It happens to lots of kids. Ten per cent."

"Jees, mate."

Confiding in Smudge was turning out to be not such a good idea. Best friends can be merciless. Gloom and self-pity engulfed me. I was so preoccupied with my own misery I was scarcely aware of Smudge coming to sit next to me on the bed. He was saying something other than "Jees, mate," but it took several seconds for the words to arrange themselves with any meaning in my overcast mind. I sat up with a jolt when I realized he'd said:

"Ain't ya gonna show me it?"

"Show you . . . ?" I looked at Smudge with patent disbelief. I think my mouth was hanging open. He seemed to be his old self, grinning a mile wide.

"But . . . but, it's on my . . . um, dick."

"I know. Ya said."

"I don't . . . I can't . . ."

"We're mates. It's okay."

"I don't think so."

"C'mon. I ain't never seen one."

"I can't . . ." I wanted to, but I couldn't. My heart was pounding. I couldn't decide whether I was excited or scared. In all our years of close and constant friendship, Smudge had never seen my cock, nor I his. It had simply never happened. I sometimes felt as though we'd deliberately gone out of our way to make sure it didn't happen. Many times, pissing in the school toilets, standing breathlessly shoulder to shoulder, I'd strained my eyeballs in their sockets to catch a sideways glimpse of his dangling cock. Often, I sensed he was doing the same. On these occasions, I was tempted to move my hand away, shift a little, swivel my hips, to bring my cock into view. But as he'd never moved his hand, turned his hips or head, I hadn't either.

"C'mon, mate. Giss a look. Please," he was saying, and I

decided I was both scared *and* excited. Ever since I'd known Smudge I'd dreamed of something like this happening. At night, with my hard cock in my hand, I would try to picture him lying beside me, his body naked, his cock as thickly risen and urgently in need as mine. We would jack off together, side by side with our bodies warmly connected, and after a while I'd reach for him and he'd take mine in his hand and our hands would squeeze and stroke until . . . but when I shot my load, I did it alone into an old outgrown football sock. Most nights I faded into sleep with the smell of fresh cum in my nostrils and Smudge fresh on my mind.

"Please, mate. Just a little look. Please." His squinting eyes were glued on my well-filled crotch like a little boy's eyes glued on a fresh-filled biscuit tin. "Please . . ." His face was glowing with enthusiasm, urgent and pleading, and my resistance was eroding under his unyielding perseverance. My self-doubts and second-thoughts receded behind an inrush of self-esteem. I no longer felt wary, hesitant. I felt confident, almost important. My forehead smoothed and my chest expanded, my legs pushed out straight and my thighs flexed. I let down my guard and threw caution to the wind. I would do it. I would show him my wart. My cock.

"All right," I said, abruptly, with a hint of exasperation. "If you're going to make such a huge fuss about it."

His expression instantly assumed a mixture of gleeful satisfaction for the battle won and horrified surprise that it had been won at all. I think capitulation was the last thing he expected of me. He was taken aback, totally unprepared, as scared as I'd been a few minutes earlier.

"Are ya . . . are ya *sure?*" he blurted out.

"Yeah," I said off-handedly, relaxing back on the bed. I didn't want to seem too willing so I added, "Pretty sure."

"Crikey, mate. Ya don't have to. I mean . . ."

"It's all right," I said, drawing my hands up my thighs, running my fingers around the bulge between my legs, watching his narrow-slitted catlike eyes follow my lingering figure-eight passes. He was caught, hook, line and sinker. "You said you'd never seen one. Now's your chance."

"Okay," he said, without much conviction.

"Okay," I said, with even less.

Now that a showing of the wart had been agreed on, neither of us knew what to do next. We sat on the bed, perfectly still and quiet, gazing intently at the wall opposite as if we might find the instructions on how to proceed printed there.

"So?" I asked, finally. I was getting impatient, more with myself than with Smudge.

"So what?" he said. Also impatient.

"Do you want to see it or not?"

"I already said I did, didn't I?"

"Well. Then look."

"Whaddya think I got? X-ray vision or something?"

"Oh. Yeah. Sorry." My cheeks flushed with embarrassment. Agreeing to be a party to a wart inspection was, in itself, not enough. I was obliged to make the afflicted organ available, expose it to the light of day (and Smudge's ogling eyes) for close scrutiny. I fumbled with my belt buckle. My fingers were all thumbs. Whatever was about to happen, I knew, for both of us, was going to be more profoundly enlightening, more drastically revealing than merely looking at a wart. Much much more. This realization sent a stream of lively images to my already overloaded brain. I felt an erection coming on from way down in my pelvis. It grabbed and squeezed the tip of my spine before it slowly pumped its power into my cock. Despite my silent cries of protest, my reticent penis was jerked out of an innocent slumber and forced up into a position of alert complicity. Its hoped-for role as an impartial bystander was not to be. Straining the fabric of my jeans, making the buttons almost impossible to undo, it pounded now in anxious anticipation. And I was getting nowhere—but flustered—fast.

"Can I help?" Smudge offered cautiously, taking note of my ineffectual fingers.

"No! No!" I grimaced, aghast at such an intimate suggestion. But my cock liked the idea. It expanded further and throbbed, tightening the material at my crotch, filling out any remaining slack so that I had no leverage at all anymore on the buttons.

"Looks like ya dick's got hard." He was grinning from ear to ear, prurient interest having dispelled recent qualms.

I turned my head and flung a cold stare at him.

"It has not," I snapped. Then seeing there was overwhelming evidence to support his claim, I tried a different tactic. "Actually, you're right. The stupid thing is always doing that. Ha. ha." My attempt at light-hearted laughter failed so I switched to a businesslike tone. "We'd better wait till it goes down, I spose."

"No fear, mate. Get it out. Let's see it."

"I thought it was the wart you wanted to see."

"Yeah! Yeah! That's right. The wart, mate." Smudge's face was aglow and his thinking rational. "It'll be easier to see, if yer dick's good an' hard."

"I dunno..." I faltered. But he was right. Having observed the wart under all conditions—including in the bathtub, under water—it was definitely easier to see when my cock was fully distended and upstanding.

"Stand up," he ordered. His earlier eagerness and aplomb had returned as quickly as mine had faded. There wasn't any bluff left in me. I stood up without contention or complaint.

"Undo them buttons."

The undoing wasn't easy, but I did it.

"Drop ya duds."

I looked at the ceiling and wriggled my jeans down over my hips. I wasn't wearing underpants. I felt worn denim slither down my bare legs and bunch loosely at my ankles. I heard Smudge's intake of breath and a slow exhaling through-the-teeth whistle.

"Crikey, it's a beaut, mate."

"It's ugly..." I said to the ceiling.

"Fuck no, mate. It's a real beauty."

"It's ugly, and it's..."

"It's fuckin' beautiful," he interrupted.

"It's... it's" And then it struck me that it was my cock he was so eloquently admiring. After several more whistles and utterances of unabashed appreciation, he said, "So where's the famous wart?"

Without looking down, I pointed to the left side of my cock midway.

"Oh yeah. I see it. Shit, mate, it's real little. Just a bit of a bump. Like a little brown tit."

The dictionary's definition came to mind; Smudge's modest brain wasn't the first to conjure up a wart and nipple likeness.

"Can I touch it?"

"Hell, no!"

But he wasn't asking for permission; his fingers were already on my cock. And they weren't touching the wart, they were nimbly encircling my rigid shaft.

"I said no!" I yelled.

"Massage is the best treatment for these little fuckers," he said with doctor-to-patient seriousness, pumping his fisted hand up and down the length of my astounded cock.

"No!" I yelled.

"Shut the fuck up during treatment," he snarled.

My pleading cries of "No! No!" became whimpers of "Oh! Oh!" as he expertly whisked away. His hand on my cock felt so much better than my own had ever felt. At first, I thought he was using a technique I had not yet discovered, but when I looked down at the masturbating fist it dawned on me that it wasn't *how* he was doing it, it was *because* he was doing it that caused the incredible excitement, the devastating pleasure. The head of my cock was swollen, bloated up bigger than I'd ever seen it, inflamed a deep purplish-red and frothing at the mouth.

"Oh... Oh... Oh..." I gasped.

"Yeah... Yeah... Yeah..." he echoed, urging me on. His other hand was busy at his own crotch, flipping buttons out of buttonholes. The front of his jeans veed open and fingers squirmed inside. Then his cock was outside, fully erect, his left hand flashing along it at the exact same demonic speed his right hand worked on me. Straining to see more, wanting to see all of it, I could catch only fleshy glimpses of its thick shaft. A fiery liquid heat radiating out from the pit of my stomach buckled my knees and blurred my vision. I could see nothing in focus yet I was experiencing everything with an intense clarity.

"Yeah . . . Yeah . . . Yeah . . ." Smudge's deep-throated chant reverberated through the echo chamber of my mind. I knew I was dangerously close to orgasm. My balls were tightening up, gathering and contracting in preparation for the inevitable, uncontrollable release of sperm. I had to warn him.

"It's coming. Oh, fuck! I'm gonna cum . . . cummm . . ." My desperate cry hummed and died in my throat, silenced by a great sickening explosion in my bowels. My cock inflated to vast dimensions in his hammering hand, then it too exploded.

"Yeah . . . Shoot it . . . Shoot it . . . Shoot the fucking stuff . . . ," Smudge was growling as I squirted long silvery ropes of cum into the air. Warm splashes on my bare legs told me he was shooting too.

As our gut-grabbing spasms slowly faded, I became aware of cool air caressing my sweaty descending ball sac. The room and Smudge gradually came back into focus. The smell of fresh semen wafted heady and rich about us. Splattered cum patterned the front of his shirt like embroidery; milk-white coagulations snaking viscously over coal-black grease stains. There were gobs of trickling cum on my legs from my thighs to my ankles.

Everything had happened so unexpectedly, so impulsively, I wondered how we would return to who we were, what we would say to each other, how we would explain this terrible, wonderful thing that had overtaken us without forethought or warning. I moved back a step, guardedly, as Smudge rose to standing, not knowing what to expect from him, trying to think of something significant, something deeply meaningful to say. Something, anything; to justify, to absolve.

He looked at me grimly, shrugged, then broke into a smile; the same easy wide-open smile he greeted me with every day. "We're still good mates, ain't we?"

I nodded, returning his infectious smile with an embarrassed version of my own.

"No worries, then," he said, reaching down for the droplet

pearling the head of my overcurved cock, touching his cummy fingertip to the tip of my nose, taking it to the tip of his tongue. Then chuckling, "Your wart's a beaut."

Before I had a chance to release my sucked-in breath, he'd tucked in his cock, done up his jeans and was gone with a graceful vault through the window.

* * *

THE NEXT DAY AT SCHOOL Smudge seemed to be his usual self. I was wary at first, minding my p's and q's, but when it was obvious there wasn't the slightest change in his behavior toward me, I relaxed. It was as though what had happened yesterday had never happened at all. That is, until recess. When we raced each other to the lavatories and stood side by side, shoulder-shoving and out of breath, there was a difference, an intimacy, in the way we positioned ourselves. He stared openly at my cascading cock and I ogled his without any sense of guilt or embarrassment. We both swiveled our hips for a common view. I flinched but stood my ground when his bold fingers reached to touch the wart side of my cock.

"Has it gone yet?" he asked. We watched my cock respond to the warmth of his question.

"Not yet," I said, feeling fortunate in some perverse way to be able to admit that it was still with me.

"Come over to my place after school." Smudge balanced my cock's thickened shaft in his palm, weighing it appreciatively. "For some more treatment," he said, with a sly wink. He bounced my half-hard in his hand and shook his own suggestively. "Jake stayed over last night," he explained as we buttoned up, "and he showed me this great way to get rid of the nasty little bastards."

"Okay," I grinned, and my happy cock bucked harder, remembering yesterday's treatment. (Smudge was the youngest of the four Lawson boys and the only one still living at home. Jake, the second youngest, turned up now and then when he wasn't on the road with his biker mates or in jail.)

I finished my homework in record time that afternoon,

aware for the first time in my life that sex was the ultimate motivator. I dashed off a three-page essay on my favorite exploration in Australian history: the infamous Burke and Wills expedition of 1860, an abortive, fatal, though highly colorful attempt at a south-north crossing of the continent. Then I biked over to Smudge's, pedaling with the speed of the essayist, and considerably more style.

I always rang the Lawson's doorbell first even though I knew it didn't work. Every time I pressed the wobbly button there was the possibility it might have been fixed since the last time. Then I knocked.

An ovoid mass loomed into the shadowy space behind the sagging screen door. "He ain't in 'ere," Smudge's mum said and stood to fill the doorway. "Try round the back."

As I stepped off the dry-rotted veranda she called after me. "If ya see the lazy bugger tell 'im the bloody garbage ain't been took out in donkey's years."

Smudge was in the back yard patching a leak in his bicycle tire. The bike stood with its wheels in the air, the inner tube on the rear wheel yanked out like the intestines of a slaughtered sheep, cancerous with lumpy patches. My enthusiasm and semi-distended mmber shrank instantly at the sight of the tube's wart-like repairs. I began to back away but he heard my crunch on the gravel path and looked up with a grin that pulled his upper lip back over his teeth like an aggressive chimpanzee.

"Ready for the cure?" he smirked, submerging the lowest length of tube in a chipped enamel basin of dirty water.

I glanced around nervously and made awkward arabesques in the dusty gravel with the toe of my sneaker. "I s'pose so..." I muttered, chin down and squinty-eyed.

"It's guaranteed to get results." His front teeth were still bared as he twisted the inner tube in his big hands, causing it to hiss and bubble in the basin. I couldn't stop staring at his teeth. They seemed unusually large when seen in their entirety, exposed to the gums. I wondered if they were more yellow than white because he smoked a pack of cigarettes a day. I wondered if his brother Jake really knew a cure for warts.

"Jake's a bloody expert. He taught me real good." His upper lip gradually fell back into place and he bent over the basin, clamping his fists around the inner tube's slithery body. He said nothing more, confident that nothing more need be said. I watched his strong agile hands as they worked with experienced movements, imagining my cock as the painstakingly manipulated inner tube. When he was finished he pumped up the tire and gave the wheel an easy slap to set it spinning. He walked into the shed, beckoning me to follow with a terse tilt of the head.

"Drop yer strides," he said gruffly, over his shoulder.

"What?" My disbelief stopped me dead in my tracks at the shed door.

"You 'eard. Take yer bloody jeans off." He grabbed my shoulder, hauled me inside and wrestled with the jerry-built door to close it behind us. I was about to argue but the sad wheezing sigh of the door's rusted hinges and the dull resounding thud of the wooden latchpole dropping into place were sounds of such abject finality that protest seemed pointless. Feeling sacrificial, I resigned myself to whatever Fate and Smudge had in store for me.

Except for the white-hot cracks around the door there was no light. The blackness was thickened by the rich and heady smells of dank earth, sump oil and fecal decay. I could hear Smudge unbuckling his belt, so I did what he did, turning away from him in the darkness to lower my jeans. As my eyes adjusted to the dimness I could make out the skeletal shapes of broken furniture, haphazard piles of crates and lumber, the ruined carcasses of motorbikes, and Smudge standing in profile, stark naked, his body edged in filtered bister light. His cock was jutting away from the concave curve of his belly, vibrantly erect and menacingly huge.

"Take everything off," he said.

"Okay, boss," I said, turning to face him, trying to hide my self-consciousness and insecurity behind a show of bravado. "Not my socks, though."

"Every bloody thing," he said.

"What about ants? And spiders?"

"Fuck 'em."

"Okay, okay. Everything then." I hoped the right sentiments were there in my voice: confidence, boldness, grateful anticipation. In reality my stomach was doing somersaults. My brain was a kaleidoscope of question marks, not at all convinced I was ready for big brother Jake's wonder cure. My cock, however, was not having the same misgivings. My shit-for-brains cock had no worries. Almost perpendicular in front of my fluttery stomach, it stood proud and tall in eager expectation.

As I balanced on one foot and then the other to pull off my socks, hopping like a rheumaticky roo, I felt Smudge's eagle eyes appraising my body.

"C'mon over 'ere, mate," he said, solicitously, taking my arm, moving me through the yellowish oily half-light. "Park ya bum on that." I was guided down onto what appeared to be a bench seat from a lorry. The creaky vinyl upholstery was sharply cold on my bare flesh at first, but as it warmed it became softly pliant and surprisingly comfortable.

"Nice and comfy?" Smudge asked as he dropped to his knees between my outspread legs.

"Mmmm," I replied, relaxing back, then jumped when I felt his hands on my thighs.

"Easy, boy. Easy," Smudge crooned, and his hands were warm and caressing on my trembling thighs. My heart was galloping. My cock was so hard it seemed a stranger to my body, independent and self-assured. His hands slid slowly upward. My balls tingled to the first delicate touch and throbbed to a firmer grip. He cupped them in turn, squeezing gently, rolling them from hand to hand. Thick fingers lightly traveled the length of my cock and circled its girth; a big sweaty-palmed fist closing purposefully around my throbbing shaft.

He looked up at me, looking into my face with his mouth half open, his eyes half closed, expressing a concentration so deep it resembled a trance. I watched him watching me, his eyes searching for answers to questions he would never dare ask. Holding me captive with his dreamy hypnotic gaze he moved his head forward, forward and down. His tongue flashed between dark lips and emerged cobra-like, extending with reptilian intent to touch the wart on the side of my cock with its glistening pointed tip. I heard my breath catch in my throat. The tongue recoiled, then extended again. It jabbed and flicked and lathed, sending waves of indescribable pleasure through my body. Then something quite bizarre and wonderful happened that caused me cry out aloud, "Oh, bloody hell!" The whole head of my cock had been taken into the burning cavern of his mouth. He held it there, squeezing it with his tongue and cheeks while I gasped in amazement and delight.

Inch by inch he consumed my slickened shaft until my tormented cockhead forced his throat open. It didn't seem possible, but the entire length of my cock felt as if it had been swallowed. Smudge put his hands on my chest and without taking his mouth off my cock pushed me back until I was lying spreadeagled along the bench. He adjusted his kneeling position and set to work in earnest with lips and tongue and suctioning throat. I pushed up my hips and held his rhythmically bobbing head in my hands in case he might think my groaning meant I wanted him to stop.

Stopping was the last item on Smudge's agenda, having just begun a treatment that required him to suck as many loads out of the patient as the patient was ready and willing to let him have. I gave him two big ones and a smaller dribbler before I shoved him away half an hour later. "I need a breather," I gasped, struggling to sit upright on the bench seat.

"Aw, jees, mate. Don't be a spoilsport."

"How can we be sure . . . doing this . . . is doing any good?" I asked between breaths.

"It's bloody doin' me a lotta good, I know that," he grinned. "C'mon, let's 'ave another little taste."

"Fair go," I said, slapping his hand off my wilted dick. "Keep your dirty big oversexed paws to yourself."

"Jees, mate, I'm only doin' it for yer health's sake." Smudge's contrition was not convincing.

"Your brother told you doing this... er, I mean, putting it in your mouth... gets rid of warts."

"S'right."

"How?"

"The spit in yer mouth, see. It's nature's medicine," he said, puffed up with instant importance. "Ya seen dogs lickin' their dicks, aintcha?"

I nodded.

"Ever seen warts on a dog's dick then?"

I shook my head, not thinking about dogs but thinking about his brother. About his three brothers. "You've done this before," I said with forceful accusation. "You've done it with your brothers."

"S'right." His response was offhand, casual.

"Much?"

"Since I can remember."

"Bloody hell!" I said, "I never knew..."

"Ya never asked, mate. Didya?" He was laughing, pushing me backwards across the well-worn upholstered bench. "Time for another dose of the medicine." And his head dipped down to my crotch and I found myself once again engulfed in wetness and heat and excruciating pleasure.

* * *

THE NEXT MORNING, a Tuesday, there were two warts, not one.

"I'm done for," I told myself with sinking despair, retying the cord of my pajama pants with a vengeance, banishing my guilty member from sight.

I made a determined effort to broach the subject of warts again at the breakfast table. Using a less direct approach than the previously unsuccessful attempt, I said, perhaps a trifle too theatrically: "I dreamt I got swept out to sea at Bondi Beach."

"Bondi?" Mum's penciled eyebrows formed perfect twin arches.

"Well, no. Actually it was Bilgola," I corrected myself, relocating my dream to a more acceptable, less middle-class-touristy locale.

"Bilgola, Bunny Rabbit. Of course." She smiled vacantly, daintily spearing a deviled kidney.

"I dreamt this lifesaver thrashed out in record time to pull me in."

"Hmm. That's nice, dear."

"He gave me mouth-to-mouth, and as I lay recovering in the sand I couldn't help noticing the warts." I paused for a breath and pitched my voice down an octave. "He had warts all over his feet."

"Hmm?" Tiny furrows disturbed Mum's otherwise flawless brow.

"Warts all over his feet," I repeated with dramatic resonance. Dad stopped eating. He looked at me, looked at Mum, then looked at the ceiling.

"How awful, dear," Mum said, looking at Dad, who had resumed eating.

"If he'd *really* saved me, in real life, I mean... Is there a way to repay him, some way to get rid of his warts, maybe? I mean, as a reward."

"I don't know I'm sure, dear," Mum said, anxious to disinvolve herself from such unpleasantness. But Dad's attention had been captured. He sat back, flicked his serviette across his pin-striped knees, and delivered a boardroom announcement:

"The last time a lifesaver saved you from bloody drowning I donated a thousand pounds to the Lifesaving Club."

After an appropriately businesslike silence, I said with corporate clarity, "You don't need to this time, Dad. It was only a dream."

"He was dreaming again, dear," Mum explained to Dad, apologetically.

"What about the warts?" I heard the urgency in my plea for help.

"What warts, dear?"

"The lifesaver's." But my despair went unheard.

"He doesn't have any, Bunny Rabbit. You dreamed them."

"I'll send the Club a check when I get to the office," Dad said, folding his serviette precisely, pushing his chair away from the table. "Just in case."

"In case?" Mum asked.

"In case the silly bugger wasn't dreaming."

"I was . . . I was . . ." I stammered, fighting back tears of frustration. "I *was* dreaming . . ."

"You can't bloodywell see warts in a dream," Dad said in a tone of voice that closed all further conversation. I felt some vague consolation knowing that my two warts were valued—in Dad's bank-ledger method of accounting for life, at least—at five hundred pounds apiece.

At school that day Smudge was the same old easygoing no-worries Smudge he always was while I teetered on the brink of nervous collapse. I tried in vain on several occasions to draw him aside to whisper my dreadful news. A hastily scrawled note I attempted to pass to him in geography class—which read: I HAVE TWO! HELP!—was intercepted by Pauline Griffiths, who, having a mad pash for me, assumed it was my long-awaited reciprocation.

"Two what?" she mouthed as fetchingly as any girl with buck teeth in braces can mouth.

"Er. Two, um . . . two egg salad sandwiches."

The look of instant disapointment that crossed her bland pudding face carried the message of her fortunate distaste for egg salad sandwiches. Smudge, needless to say, remained infuriatingly oblivious to this unrequited interchange.

It wasn't until I was receiving "the treatment" in the Lawson's backyard shed, reclining shirtless and pantless on the bench seat from one of their lately-dead lorries, my afflicted member securely lodged in the gullet of their youngest son, that I finally blurted out:

"There's two now."

Smudge looked up at me, unblinking, his eyes glassy and slightly askew. Beads of sweat, tiny as dew drops, slid unhindered down his bulging cheeks. He made a low humming noise at the back of his throat, lowered his lids, and resumed sucking. Shortly after that he hummed again and gulped as I squirted a sizable load into deep and vibrating warmth.

"Two, ya say." He settled back on his haunches to stare at me, saying incredulously, "Garn, yer shittin' me."

"Two, side by side," I said dejectedly, slipping into a post-orgasmic depression.

He ran his tongue over his top lip, like a milk-thirsty calf. "No worries," he grinned, "we'll just double the treatment." The grin developed into one of his out-of-control smiles showing dark pink gums. Slouching forward, he nuzzled my damp belly, popped my deflated dribbling cock back into his mouth and started a repeat performance with unbridled enthusiasm.

"Er, Smudge... ah, if you don't mind," I said politely, "it sort of hurts when you suck so hard right after I cum."

He released my cock, reluctantly, looking like a baby who's been yanked off its mother's tit. "Yer batteries need to recharge a bit, I s'pose," he offered wistfully, before his face was brightened by an alternative thought. "I know, mate. Why dontcha suck me for a while?"

"Weeell... I don't know..." I faltered. His offer took me by surprise. I was dying to suck his big chunky-thick cock, had been all along, but I didn't want to seem overanxious.

"C'mon, matey. Just a little bit. Till ya get yer steam back up. C'mon."

"But you don't have warts on... on yours." My fingers were crossed that he wouldn't be swayed by my reasoning.

"Don't matter." He wasn't. "You can do it so's I won't get none." And his reasoning was so much more astute than mine. "A suck-ounce of prevention's better'n a pound of cure." This Smudge-colored variation on a time-worn platitude propounded a philosophy I had no argument with. I struggled only briefly with temptation, then abandoned my phony reticence.

"Okay," I said, sliding off the bench. "If you really think it'll help."

"No fear, mate. It's a dead cert." Smudge's face lit up like a beacon, radiating as much lustful anticipation as I felt. We changed places, our bodies weaving a naked not-ungraceful pas de deux, and I snuggled between his robust smooth-muscled thighs, settling in as happily as a homing pigeon come to roost.

My best mate's rampant penis was breathtakingly beautiful, a real corker of a cock. I'd not had a chance to get a firsthand close-up sighting during our wild whirligig days of wart purging. (Though recent, all that had happened so suddenly, so unexpectedly, and still remained so thrillingly inexplicable.) Now here it was, a veritable bobby-dazzler, inches from my nose which was busier than a pointing foxhound's, twitching and whiffing away at the bevy of beguiling boycock smells.

I scooted forward to let its glowing head brush my lips. A small ooze of liquid bubbled out, not clear but thick and milky. I took it with my tongue and recognized the taste.

"You've cum already?" I asked, looking up with mild astonishment. Genuinely curious.

Smudge was splayed out like a floppy starfish: lissome arms extended, resting loosely along the back of the seat, his limp-necked head lolling over the edge, eyes heavy-lidded, mouth slack. "Course I 'ave," he mumbled, without moving a single body part, not even his lips. Then opening one eye enough to confirm the sincerity of the question in my face, he went on to explain the circumstances, smiling wryly, "Every time ya blow in me mouth I shoot the works. Don't 'ave t'give it a wank or nothin'."

"You mean, whenever I, er..."

"S'right, sport. Works like a charm, every time."

"Golly!" I said, impressed with my ability to cause him so much spontaneous excitement. Suddenly a less happy thought occurred to me. "If you've just cum, you probably don't want me to... er, do things to you."

"No worries, mate. There's plenty more where that come from. Me balls got gallons of it ready to go." The shuttered eye closed but the smile lingered. "Suck away, José."

I drew a breath, dipped my head, moistened my lips, made my mouth into a perfect O, and took what I had coming to me like a man. I thought I would be cautious, over-careful, not even much good at it the first time. But the moment my mouth engulfed his warm wet-velvet plum, something ferocious took control of me; a latent cannibal instinct drummed through my body to a rousing primal chant. "Suck. Suck. Suck. Suck," it fairly screamed. And suck I did, Jesus I did. I don't think poor old Smudge knew what hit him. Whatever he'd done with any of his three brothers, whatever mouth-to-cock sex they'd persuaded him to perform, it was instantly apparent that mine was the first genuinely enthusiastic mouth to show its unabashed appreciation of his resplendent member.

From moment one I was phenomenal. I'd been seemingly blessed with all the expertise and artful invention of a lifelong practitioner. The tricks of the trade came naturally to me. And my repertoire ran the gamut; I sucked him with the delicacy and intricate detail of a virtuoso fine-tuning a Stradivarius, and I sucked like a blood-starved vampire life-threatened by the light of dawn. He writhed, wriggled, ranted and raved, and cursed me to Hell and back and begged for mercy. He came violently, copiously, noisily, three times in quick succession; three mind-boggling, mouth-filling eruptions of syrupy-thick sweetness that came so fast I scarcely had time to gulp them down and savor their tangy residue.

"Holy fuckin' Jesus, mate. That was fuckin' marvelous," Smudge gasped, eyes slightly askew, his broad chest rising and falling rhythmically. "Sure ya ain't never done it before?"

"No, never, I replied, modestly. Then, bolstered by success and feeling immensely proud of my newfound skill, I admitted, "But I've *thought* a lot about doing it."

"With me?" Being subtle wasn't a Smudge strongpoint.

I nodded, embarrassed to say so, but flattered by the asking.

"It's always 'ere. Yours fer the askin'," he said, displaying his softening cock, offering it rudely, a flesh pink salami in his cupped hands. "Jest gimme the word when ya feel the need."

"As a preventative measure?"

"Wha...?" Smudge shot me a sideways look of puzzlement.

"To be sure you won't get warts on it," I explained.

"Yeah, yeah. S'right, mate. Jest t'be sure," he chuckled. "Better t'be sure than sorry." And he kept on intermittently chuckling as we got dressed.

* * *

A SIREN WOKE ME late in the night. I opened my eyes and wondered what time it was. I heard the sound coming closer and closer. I saw flashes of red light on the wall opposite my window. Police? Ambulance? A fire engine? The lights fluttered to a watery amber and the siren wailed itself into silence. I fell asleep and fell right into a nightmare. My cock was covered in warts. I was being paraded through the school corridors; a deformed monster, stripped naked, cast out and reviled by students and teachers alike. They jeered and mocked, likening me to a hideously endowed Phantom of the Opera, to Notre Dame's hunchback made more abhorrent by a lump-covered appendage, to a Dracula damned through all eternity with a disgusting knobby dong.

Suddenly Smudge was by my side, beating off my tormentors with his bicycle pump.

"No worries, mate. I got the perfect cure." He shouted triumphantly and the school reverberated with jubilant sound, a carillon of pealing bells.

"Come with me," he called as he strode away. My mum's glittering black car filled the corridor and prevented my following him. A sleek door opened and unseen hands jostled me into the chilling confines of powder-blue leather and mother love.

"I'll take care of you, Bunny Rabbit," the sweet voice cooed. "That's the last you'll see of him, thank goodness. The nasty horrid filthy-minded boy."

The engine hummed with malicious intent as her Daimler rolled inexorably forward to obliterate the shrinking figure of Smudge. With death in my heart I screamed a silent scream and woke, bathed in sweat. My room was bedazzled with sunshine. At first, when I ripped open my pajama bottoms, I could see nothing but yellow and green dancing spots. Then,

I saw *them.* Four warts. They loosely pinpointed the shape of a parallelogram.

"This is the end," I thought, slumping back on the bed without incentive enough to retie the pajama cord.

When I broke the dreadful news to Smudge in Geometry, the first class of the day, my frantically whispered account of the calamity seemed neither to surprise nor daunt him. He flashed his fetching grin, refusing to be infected by my moroseness, and chirped brightly and altogether too loudly:

"No worries, mate. I got the perfect cure."

Uncanny, unsavory shivers traveled the length of my spine, for those were the exact same words he'd uttered as confidently in last night's dream. But this morning there were no clamoring bells so I said, sotto voce and somewhat sarcastically, "The treatment seems to be making matters worse."

That he should stop "the treatments" was the last thing I wanted. I tried nonetheless to register a formal complaint without sounding spiteful or ungrateful. The ever-impervious Smudge, acknowledging neither my complaint nor my implied gratitude, heartily announced (upping the volume to room level), "Same time, same place, fer the treatment and the cure."

"The cure for what?" Mr. Ogilvy, our geometry teacher, asked, rotating his body the required number of degrees from the blackboard to survey a sea of attentive silence.

"The cure, I trust, for your inability to grasp that the ratio of the number to its predecessor is a constant." Mr. Ogilvy, accustomed to being greeted by vacant stares, always answered his own questions, having long ago learned it was the only way to get intelligent replies. I winced when he looked at me, then at Smudge, fearful that the purpose of our rendezvous could be read like a book on our guilty faces. But of course it could not. We presented ourselves—partners in crime since way back—as citable examples of adolescent inscrutability, and our compatriots about us were as unimpeachable, as blithely unaware as only a classroom of schoolkids can be when they know there are not-so-innocents in their ranks.

Later that day, as I leaned bodily against the shed door to

force it closed, listening to Smudge's measured breathing in the darkness, my brain conjured up images of prurient possibility and juggled the mysterious what-ifs. I tried to fathom what brother-taught quackery he'd have up his sleeve (or down his trousers) this time. When my eyes adjusted sufficiently to locate his supine form on the bench seat, he was sporting nary a sleeve or a trouser. Naked as the day he was born, he was enterprisingly engaged in paying homage to his magnificently erect cock.

"Quick! Get outta them duds an' get yer bum over 'ere," he said with deep-throated urgency. "If I flog me meat much longer I'll blow the bloody lot."

I undressed quickly, slinging my shirt and jeans across the disabled Harley I'd gotten into the habit of using as a clotheshorse. I ripped off my sneakers and socks and with an underarm throw lobbed them into the listing bassinet that, in better days, had successfully constrained all four lusty Lawson babies.

"Aaah! Christ, mate. I'm so fuckin' close," the youngest dirty-big overgrown Lawson baby was telling me. "I can't 'old on much bloody longer."

I fairly flung myself between his outstretched legs, my underpants at half-mast, not about to miss an opportunity for a mouthful of Smudge's yummy boycream. Wrapping my lips around his cock's engorged head, I slid my mouth down the heavy shaft, loving the bumpiness of the vascular ridges that networked its length and breadth.

"Oooh, Jeesuss . . ." he hissed. And the unstoppable process of orgasm overtook him. His hips fucked upwards burying his convulsing cock, rooting it deeply into my wide-open mouth. All I could hear, as bursts of flooding warmth filled my throat, was my mum's cajoling voice at mealtimes when I left food on the plate: "All of it, dear. Eat it all up. Think of the starving children in Asia."

"Fuck 'em," I thought, gulping greedily, "I'm a starving kid, too."

When Smudge's crisis was over, I dipped my face to his still-heaving belly to polish off the last few dribbles.

"Bugger me, mate," he giggled, "ya got more suck than Mum's fuckin' Hoover."

"A growing boy needs all the nourishment he can get," I said to his gloppy navel before I slurped the cum out of it.

"Ya'll need some of that for yer dick, ya silly galoot."

"My dick? Why, what for?"

"T'get it nice an' slippery, that's bloody what for."

"Why?"

"So's ya can stick it up me bumhole."

"Up... your... er, bumhole..." I stammered in utter disbelief.

"S'right. It's the cure I was tellin' ya about," he said, matter-of-factly, rolling back and swinging his legs up, knees to shoulders. He pointed to the brown wrinkled slit now so alarmingly exposed. "Ya bung it in 'ere," he grinned lewdly, "for the perfect cure."

"But, that's... that's impossible." I was gaping open-mouthed, fascinated by the tiny moist eye that Smudge made wink at me. "You must be bonkers to think my dick will fit in your... er, in there."

"Course it bloody will, mate, I've 'ad Jake's up there more times than I've 'ad hot dinners. No trouble at all. Piece a cake. An' his is bigger'n yours an' mine put together."

I paused to digest this curious information and collect my thoughts, harboring a sudden need to have hands-on knowledge of his brother's allegedly oversized penis. I also needed confirmation of the effectiveness of the bizarre act he was asking me to perform. I posed a cautious question: "Jake said putting a dick in your... er, in there... will cure warts?"

"Every time," he said. "It's guaranteed. It's... it's invallible."

"Infallible," I corrected, not entirely reassured.

"Yeah, that too."

"But I can't understand how..."

"C'mon, mate. Be a sport," Smudge interrupted. "Stop beating around the bush and stick the fucker in. It'll be good for ya, and it even *feels* good."

"It does?" I had to admit the thought of inserting my dick

into that cute little hole was beginning to intrigue me. My cock, as usual, was ready to try anything.

"Jake ses bumholes are a lot tighter'n twats. 'E loves 'em. Won't 'ardly fuck anything else anymore. The randy bastard's sniffin' round mine the minute 'e walks in the door."

"Golly!" I said, appalled and amazed by these revelations.

"C'mon, sport. Give it a burl."

It was clear to me Smudge was determined to have me go through with this unorthodox cure, so with one of my elaborate eyes-rolling, arms-akimbo gestures, I said, feigning exasperation, "Oh, all *right.*"

"Spit on yer dick first but, so's it'll go in easier."

Heaving a sigh of resignation and relief, I swirled my tongue around the inside of my mouth, spat a copious glob of cummy saliva into my palm and thoroughly anointed my cock.

"I'm ready," I said, politely.

"Jesus Christ, ya don't need t'buy a bloody ticket. Stick it in."

"Okay." I gave him a nervous smile as I crouched over his beefy thighs, aiming my intrepid cock toward previously uncharted territory an inch or so below his heavy-hanging balls. Bingo. The blunt tip of my saliva-slick dick connected fair and square in the middle of his anxious squinting eye. When Smudge felt the press of it, tentative though it was, he began babbling directions on how to proceed:

"Yeah! That's it, mate. Hit the jackpot. Good. Now push a bit. Good. That's the way. Now a bit more." I pushed harder. "Aargh! That's too much. Ease off a bit. Yeah, that's it. Good. Now, real slow, push some more. Yeah. Good. Easy does it. Yeah." I bore down slowly, ever-so-slowly, aware of a gradual sort of springy elastic giving way. "Yeah, oh yeah, mate. That's the way. That's good. Yer doin' great. Keep it up. Keep pushin' just like that. Yeah, that's it, mate. Keep pushin' in. Yeah. All the way, José."

With my eyes closed to better concentrate, interpreting his instructions as best I could, I pushed, pulled and paused obediently on command. And that's how I first penetrated my best friend's bumhole: going in on a wing and a prayer, sightless and foggy-brained, guided in by ground control.

When his signals began to make less and less sense and he was mumbling things like, "Hmmm... Thassnice, sooo nice... Oooaaah... Hmmm," I opened my eyes and looked down between our coupled bodies. I couldn't contain a small cry of astonished surprise: "Oh!" My cock had almost entirely disappeared—was buried but for a meager inch—inside his clenching ass.

"Hmmm... Feels nice in there, don't it?" he said, wriggling his bottom lasciviously.

I grunted my approval and pushed and pulled with increasing enthusiasm. It felt more than *nice.* It was undoubtedly the most wonderful, the most sinfully exquisite sensation I'd ever experienced. Each successive movement stimulated, aroused, inflamed me more than the one before. Liquid pleasure rose in me like spring-risen sap and surged through my body, inciting in me an irresistible need to thrust faster and deeper.

"Oh, yeah. That's it. That's fuckin' it. Gimme it good an' deep," Smudge groaned as I drove my insatiable cock into his hot receptive asshole. "Oh, yeah. Fuck me. Ram that big fuckin' dick all the way in."

My technique improved and my tempo increased and intensified as he urged me on. "Deeper... Deeper..." His hands gripped my buttocks to haul me in to the utmost at each downward plunge. "Fuck me... Fuck me... Fuck me," he grunted in rhythm with my inward-slamming assault. I could hear wet slapping sounds and suctioning squelches as I worked my swollen cock in and out. There were sounds, too, coming from my open mouth: not words but mumbled mewling sobs.

Smudge knew before I did that I'd passed the point of no return, that I was at the churning threshold of orgasm. Enfolding me with his arms and legs, locking me tightly to his arched body, he growled, "Shoot it in me. Fuckin' fill me up." My cock jerked almost all the way out of him, then rammed back home with a powerful desperate finality that made us both cry out. My violently spasming cock squirted into him, ejaculating with an intensity I would never have thought possible. A rush of sticky wetness between our frictioning bellies told me he was shooting too. In those precious seconds of shared climax we spewed out our loads together, uncontrollably voicing the agony of our release with choked-out profanities and strangled cries.

During a mindless daze that followed, disentangling myself from limbs that fell away limp and ineffectual, I somehow slithered down his body to tenderly and dreamily claim the smeared juices that shimmered on the curves and hollows of his belly and groin. And later still, and wordless, Smudge gently guided me to another corner of the shed where he had me lie back—lumpily cushioned by the musty folds of threadbare carpet—and knelt at my side to re-erect my flaccid cock with deliberate and sensual mouthings.

When he had me throbbing and rigid, my cock pointing to the rafters like a stubby flagpole, he cocked a limber leg and straddled my hips. Keeping my vertical cock on course with a terse finger and thumb, he ever-so-slowly lowered himself, descending in the duration of one sustained sigh of contentment, sinking and settling until he was completely impaled.

The second fuck was as fabulous as the first, yet as different in direction as warp and weft. And if his bumhole seemed hotter the second time round, it wasn't as tight and certainly a lot sloppier; it trickled a secondhand load from the previous cumming into my dick hair and down my balls. Whereas the first fuck had been accomplished mainly through my efforts, this time Smudge did all the work. Comfortably prone and smugly pleasured, I clenched my carpet-itchy bum cheeks now and again while he bounced and bucked and yahooed like a poncy rodeo cowboy.

Cumming was as slow to arrive as Second Comings are known to be, but I did see the same fiery starbursts and hollered the same vocal accompaniments. We didn't quite manage a mutual shooting. Though damnably close, he was still furiously jerking when I started to unload inside him and I could see his cock was red-hot bloated and almost there.

"Let me have it," I pleaded, pumping the last piddling spurts into his bowels. My begging mouth locked open as he readied, aimed and fired, volleying four fulsome rounds to the back of my throat. The fifth fell short and splattered my chin, and the sixth and seventh, losing momentum, made a mess on my chest. Round eight gushed over his flailing fist and nine and ten weren't much more than dribbling afterthoughts. When he dismounted I sucked his squishy dick's watery residue and squeegeed my dick with a crooked finger, sucking up and swallowing as avariciously as Asian kids into my leftovers.

"Waste not want not," I pompously confessed to Smudge in a funereal monotone, and we immediately fell into a fit of the giggles. Falling into each other's arms. Two best mates not yet comprehending the awesome significance of their joyous embrace.

* * *

THAT NIGHT, I slept a calm sleep, uninterrupted by nightmares, uncluttered with dreams. I awoke, I think, to the sound of a bird singing. The sun was still low and soft, and I could hear Mum in the rose garden snipping tall stems for the breakfast table. Without needing to look, I knew the warts were gone. All that remained—I did check, of course, scrutinizing minutely with Mum's small ivory-handled magnifying glass—were four faintest-of-faint pale dots that you'd never find unless you knew exactly where to look.

When my trembling fingers dialed the Lawsons' number I knew Smudge would be sleeping and I'd have to deal with his cantankerous mum. I braced myself to do battle, determined that he should share in the rejoicing. To my astonishment she proved to be cooperative, almost agreeable:

"Lazy bugger's still snorin' his bloody 'ead orff," she drawled, as nasal as her sons. "Hang on a sec, willya. I'll get 'im for ya."

After an interminable silence there came an unpleasant scraping noise followed by a dull, dispirited "G'day."

"It's me. I've got news," I exclaimed, scarcely able to subdue my exuberance.

Another extended silence, then, "Yeah." It was Smudge's voice but it wasn't Smudge.

"Are you all right?"

"Yeah." The voice was flat, lifeless.

"Something's the matter. What is it?"

"Nothin'."

"No, really. Something's wrong, I can tell."

"Yeah."

"What is it?" My question went softly to him through the humming wires.

"Warts."

"Warts! What warts?"

"Mine."

"Yours? You've got *warts?*"

"Yeah."

"Bloody hell! I don't believe it."

"I 'ave. Seven of the ugly fuckers. On me dick."

"Bloody hell!"

We both suffered in silence for the next few minutes. Whirring cogs and flywheels in my agitated brain were working overtime, sorting and sifting through emotional slop to line up a rational chronology of fact: I had warts. I told Smudge. He had the cure. My warts are gone. Now, Smudge has warts. He tells me. I have the . . . *that's it! I have the cure!*

Wanting to scream, I announced airily into the mouthpiece, "I have the perfect cure."

"What cure?"

"Jake's. Your brother's cure. Works like a charm every time, remember," I said, elated, mimicking his former breezy self-confident salesmanship. "I can *personally* guarantee it."

"What? Ya don't mean . . ." There was a long breathy pause. I could hear the pennies drop into the mired depths of Smudge's understanding. He said, finally, ". . . they're gone?"

"Gone."

"Holy fuckin' Jesus Christ."

"I'm on my way over. See you in the shed in twenty minutes," I told him. Then not able to resist slipping into his vernacular, I drawled, "Fuck school today, mate. Get yer dirty-big warty dick good an' hard. Me tight little bumhole's gonna be all juiced-up an' rarin' t'go."

"Are ya sure..."

"No worries today, José."

My best mate giggled.

Ginger Roger

GINGER MARCH ended his career as an orphan before his eighteenth month was up to become Roger Charles Whittington Smythe-Halliday.

Penelope and Charles Smythe-Halliday chose Ginger for his bright blue eyes and perfectly formed china-doll lips, for the peaches-and-creaminess of his complexion, for the wisps of spun gold that framed his cherubic features, for the utterly divine gurgling sounds he produced when cushiony little hands were gently squeezed. Naturally, they had no intention of retaining the name under which their precious foundling was filed at the adoption agency, it being so dreadfully common, so *plebeian.* After all, they reasoned, Ginger March was only an interim name devised by the nice people at the agency, arrived at through his having been found, literally, on their doorstep the second Monday in March (it was a toss-up for a while whether he would be March or Monday), and his head then being covered with coarse tufts of gingerish hair. (Which later, mercifully, disappeared as the soft, honeyed-blond curls grew in.)

The only other flaw the Smythe-Hallidays saw in Ginger, the one remaining tiny fly in the ointment, was the ugly flap of skin closing over the tip of his poor wee "thing." An expeditiously prearranged stop-in at the Royal North Shore Hospital on Roger's maiden voyage to their gracious neo-Georgian style home took care of what the Smythe-Hallidays considered to be an unsightly, unsanitary affliction peculiar to the lower classes.

Ginger March was not immediately successful at being an adopted child. He did not at all enjoy leading the life of Roger Charles Whittington Smythe-Halliday. Penelope and Charles, however, were immensely pleased with their latest acquisition.

In fact, being so completely preoccupied with the novelty of nurturing, they failed to notice Ginger's dislike for his new domestic arrangements; that he took no pleasure in parents, having always fared quite-nicely-thank-you without. Ginger, not yet having attained the age of reason, responding only to primal instincts, expressed his opinions the best way he knew how. He screamed blue murder. Penelope and Charles adored the ear-piercing, angry cries, the incessant wails of rage and discontent, for hadn't they been warned their darling adoptive infant would require "a little period of adjustment"?

At the age of two years and ten months, Ginger—still showing no signs of adjustment—began to cultivate the art of the tantrum. These were not mere improvised, emotional outbursts, but carefully contrived theatrical presentations that left Penelope drained and ashen and Charles reaching for the whiskey decanter. Also, at about this time, he discovered that objects could be strewn about, disassembled, hurled to the floor in splendid extravaganzas of shattering sound and mayhem. One afternoon between naps, for example, he did in a Royal Doulton jardinière complete with a flowering azalea, emptied the bottom three shelves of books—removing pages by the grubby handful—in Charles's study, and caused a collection of Staffordshire dogs to bite the dust with much éclat when he managed, on chubby tiptoe, to reach the silken fringe of the embroidered oriental runner on which they smugly sat.

At the advice of their personal family planner at the agency, Penelope and Charles cancelled their order for a darling daughter, even though now was statistically the right time for an addition to the family. It was considered that the son should come to a more equable, optimistic outlook on life before he was presented with a sister; Roger's adjustment period, puzzlingly, having far exceeded the norm. Penelope gave silent consideration to the possibility that their precious infant—like poorly-made third-world merchandise—may have come with a basic personality defect. Charles likewise wondered if they had bought a lemon.

For his fifth birthday, the Smythe-Hallidays had Roger's nursery redecorated in pale turquoise blue with masculine magenta accents. (It had previously been duck-egg blue with daffodil yellow accents.) As the joyful fulfillment of parenting had long since palled, they hired a Mrs. McTaggert, a retired powder-room attendant from the Hotel Australia who had eighteen grandchildren and impeccable references, as a live-in nanny. Ginger felt comfortable at once with Mrs. McTaggert as she carried about her ample person certain odors and auras that were reminiscent of his earlier, happier life.

Mrs. McTaggert encouraged in Roger (did she know, with her Mother Earth intuition, he was Ginger?) an ingenious strategy for coping with the alien world about him by annexing little bits and pieces of it, its trivia, into his own private domain. The top two compartments of his room-size toy cupboard—painted fire-engine red with his initials RCWSH spanning the full-height double doors in cursive electric blue—were set aside specifically to house his collected agenda of simple truths, which included: a curlew egg, dried up inside and delicately speckled; a cluster of gum nuts that would rattle like miniature maracas when shaken; a piece of quartz from a creek bed, scrubbed clean to reveal crystal prisms casting myriad rainbows in the sunlight; a leaf locusts had reduced to mere filigreed lace; an unfurled condom, a motley-yellow, brittle skin that Ginger assumed had been shed by a snake (if Mrs. McTaggert knew what manner of reptile had worn it, she never let on); a cylindrical shard of pottery, probably a piece of shattered spout from a once-elegant teapot; and much, much more.

Ginger loved to play dead. He frequently found himself gunned down in battle, a hapless victim of guerrilla warfare in some equatorial jungle. Staggering, mortally wounded, into Mrs. McTaggert's room with much well-rehearsed moaning and clutching at his disemboweled body, he would collapse, convulsing, at her feet. After several choking gasps that diminished quite effectively in intensity, interspersed with spasmodic limb-twitching, he would be dead. Mrs. McTaggert would mourn him appropriately—lavishly, if her lumbago was not playing up—listing his brave exploits in battle, his posthumous awards for noble services selflessly rendered for the sake of his country. (These she knew by heart, her late husband an Anzac.) She would shed a (mock?) tear or two for his young life sacrificed, his destiny denied, the greatness that surely was in store for him cut short. During these eulogies, Ginger smiled surreptitiously, stifling giggles. Then Mrs. McTaggert would coax him back to life with a Violet Crumble Bar or a handful of Minties.

For Roger's seventh birthday, Penelope and Charles, concerned and secretly jealous that his affections seemed firmly planted in Mrs. McTaggert's generous bosom, presented him with a six-week-old Pomeranian pup, an adorable, silky ball of fluff. Ginger was entertained by the pup's incessant yipping and snuffling and wiggle-waggling for the better part of a week, but as there was nothing more to it than that—and it made a slobbeirng mockery of his playing dead—he banished it from his room.

Penelope and Charles, hurt and perplexed by Roger's sudden rejection of their gift and his continued indifference to themselves, gave their undivided attention to the care and welfare of the abandoned animal. They bought books on what to do, consulted pet-owning friends, subscribed to dog breeders' magazines. Penelope fashioned a pretty, bejeweled collar from a dismantled diamond bracelet and earring ensemble that was no longer stylish; she sautéed calves liver or lamb kidneys for its lunch and filet mignon or veal poached in cream for its dinner. Charles personally supervised the design and construction of a custom-made, neo-Georgian style kennel with Cuddles (its name) burnished in gold leaf on a plaque over the entrance.

For their efforts, they were amply rewarded. The darling little bundle of sweetness's yipping and snuffling and wiggle-waggling charmed and delighted them, amused them for hours on end. Mutual adoration abounded. No matter how they smothered it with love and affection, it yipped, snuffled, wiggle-waggled and returned their love and affection twofold. Although they did not voice their innermost thoughts on the matter, it did occur to both Penelope and Charles over the course of the ensuing months that a Pomeranian pup or two might have better served the purpose of brightening their childless home, rather than the far more complicated, problem-fraught addition of a secondhand son.

Shortly before Ginger's ninth birthday, the Smythe-Hallidays jointly agreed it was time to begin shaping Roger a little more aggressively into the kind of son and heir they desired. And so, abruptly, a period of modest happiness for all came to an end. Cuddles, having grown into a singularly unappealing dog, a spineless, grossly fat, neuroses-ridden cur, was boxed up and sent in a chauffered hire car to Charles's maiden aunt in Katoomba. Mrs. McTaggert was let go. In her room she left behind her reassuring smell and a potted wandering Jew. The new evil-odored, pointy-faced Latvian maid removed Mrs. McTaggert's smell with air freshener, and Ginger tied a black ribbon to the potplant and placed it prominently alongside the other priceless artifacts that represeneted the sum total of his life so far. Unwatered, the plant soon assumed the appearance of either a failed botany project or a successful art-class collage.

The number one priority in Penelope and Charles's plans for Roger was to steer him away from an allegiance he had recently formed with the two sons of Tom Tompkins, an uneducated, uncouth cement contractor who drank and brawled more than he cemented. Of course, there was more to it than snobbery because Ted and Tinker Tompkins—chips off the old block—were already on their way to no good. Throwing rocks through windows, slashing car tires, stealing from the local shops, the Tompkins boys were frequent visitors to the police station. Besides, they were older than Roger; Tinker was ten and a half and Ted was twelve, big for his age and already suffering from an early attack of puberty. They were unkempt, unsavory, ill-mannered and foul-mouthed, and Ginger worshipped every grimy, rough-and-tumble inch of them.

A birthday party was arranged and several suitable children were invited. Ted and Tinker came anyway, personally invited by Ginger as his guests of honor. They arrived early, unwashed, uncombed, in shabby disrepair, and could not be persuaded to leave. As they had had no first-hand experience with the art of innuendo or the subtleties of polite behavior it did not dawn on them that an attempt was being made to turn them away. At exactly ten minutes after the time printed on the invitations, the other children arrived, well-scrubbed and spiffily attired. By then, however, the party table was well on its way to being a shambles, made havoc by Ted and Tinker, with Ginger, in a state of birthday bliss, shouting approbation and encouragement. The other children tried to make the best of it, donning crêpe-paper hats, extricating the iced cupcakes squashed into the curried egg sandwiches, fishing the candles out of the fruit punch, and retreiving balled-up serviettes from the wall sconces.

The Tompkins boys, meantime, in high party spirits and egged on by Ginger, continued their rampage; tearing off paper hats, inflicting Chinese burns on the boys, pulling down the girls' bloomers, laughing and jeering and screaming obscenities until the children, thoroughly terrorized, wailing and weeping, fled from the Smythe-Halliday's once-gracious dining room.

The next morning, first thing, Penelope telephoned the adoption agency to see if Roger could be exchanged for another lad who might be better suited to their lifestyle, more moldable, more appreciative of what they had to offer. Her request was refused.

"This whole wretched business is making me ill," Charles said. "What is the matter with him? We give him everything."

"Perhaps we should be more strict," said Penelope. "Tighten the reins a bit. Make some rules."

Charles nodded, tamping tobacco down into the bowl of his meerschaum. "If I'd known things were going to be so bloody awful I'd never have adopted him."

The first item on the carefully handwritten two-page list of rules and regulations given to Roger stated that he was forbidden, from that day on, to have any contact *whatsoever* with the Tompkins family. Ginger did not read any further. His body had gone rigid. As the perfumed sheets of paper fluttered from his stricken fingers, there came a strange whirring inside his brain. He heard a soft crying sound that grew and grew, becoming more insistent, more vibrant, until his body was gripped and shaken by anguished screaming: "No! No! No! No!" They had taken him from his home, taken Mrs. McTaggert, now they would take his only friends. "No! No! No!" the inner voice screamed. The voice of rebellion.

Penelope and Charles felt considerably better having delivered their proclamation. They breathed mutual sighs of relief. Things were running more smoothly already, Ginger, of course, made no adjustments to the daily pattern of his existence. He spent even more time with Tinker and Ted. He felt comfortable with them; there being something about their psyches that vibrated with his, as if three tuning forks were in perfect harmony. Although they called him Rog, or more frequently Fuckface, he was, in their company, the boy he knew himself to be—Ginger March.

Using the Tompkins brothers as his inspiration, mirror images for his new self, Ginger methodically undertook the elimination of Roger Charles Whittington Smythe-Halliday. He altered the way he spoke—grammar, pronunciation, inflection, timbre, everything—to sound as Ted and Tinker did. He decreased his vocabulary's width but increased its depth by adding a plethora of filthy words. He eschewed table manners and social niceties, he affected a jaunty, loose-hipped swagger, he learned nonchalant nail-biting, sideways spitting, and nose-picking that produced visible results. All of Ted and Tinker's mannerisms, every nuance of their personalities, every devious, dirty and downright disgusting aspect of their behavior was meticulously replicated. And so, shortly before his tenth birthday, Ginger March emerged, splendidly reshaped into lower-class disreputability, a phoenix risen from the smoldering wreckage of Roger Charles Whittington Smythe-Halliday.

Penelope and Charles observed the change in Roger with growing apprehension and alarm, and yet were unable to pinpoint exactly what it was about him that was different. It was not so much what he said or did (at home, Ginger was saying and doing virtually nothing), as the vibrations that emanated from him as he moved lethargically about the house. He seemed more than just indifferent, possessing an uncanny ability to conduct his life directly and aggressively opposite to theirs. They had only to enter a room he was in for them to immediately feel it bristling with antagonism against them. If he did answer a question, some casual pleasantry in passing, he left Penelope and Charles feeling as though they had been spat on, trampled in muck and mire. When Penelope asked him if he would like a party for his tenth birthday, he slouched out of the room, muttering, "Piss on that for a joke."

Ginger acquired new skills daily. Although he was scholasticaly superior, when it got down to life's nitty-gritty it was Ted and Tinker who *knew* things, who unerringly guided him out of the marble halls of the Smythe-Halliday mansion into the earthy byways of the real world, who initiated him into preadolescent boyhood, opening the door to a fascinating array of subterfuge, mateship and forbidden pleasures. Under their robust tutelage he learned how to smoke cigarettes, how to drown cats, how to drink beer, how to pick locks, how to wring chickens' necks, how to fart on call in two different keys, and most importantly, they taught him everything a boy could want to know about sex. Ginger had suspected that the elaborate arrangement of appendages between his legs was there to serve some purpose other than peeing. Although he was delighted when they introduced him to the intriguing sensations caused by the artful manipulation of his cock and balls, he was appalled to think that doing this had not occurred to him earlier. He blamed Roger's prissiness.

Ginger made ritual observance of his tenth birthday in the company of Ted and Tinker, a happily ensconced threesome in the crawl space under the front veranda of the Tompkins' modest weatherboard bungalow. They used Ginger's pocket money (Roger received a generous weekly allowance) to buy a half-dozen bottles of Toohey's best ale, a packet of Rothmans, and a bagful of jelly beans. The jelly beans were a spur-of-the-moment purchase to add a celebratory flavor to the occasion, which otherwise would have been like any other after-schoool afternoon when the three of them retreated to

speeds, applying different pressures until, "Aaah, jees, yer a nexpert," Ted moaned, and let fly with another three gobs of cum which Ginger intercepted mid-flight with his free hand and fed to Tinker. "Ta much," slurped Tinker, who loved fresh boycream more than beer or black jelly beans or Sunday's roast lamb.

Before dinner that evening, when the maid complained about the stains on Roger's new trousers, Ginger explained, "Me ice cream dribbled, but."

At the very same time, in the front drawing room downstairs, Charles was telling Penelope, "I can't stand it any longer. It's really making me ill. They should have warned us about things like this."

"It's not our fault he's so . . . so beastly," commiserated Penelope. "It isn't as if he is our own flesh and blood. I can't possibly see how we are to blame."

"He's jollywell old enough to know he's adopted," said Charles, irritably swirling the olive in his martini glass. "I'll have it out with him, man to man. See if I can get him to pull up his socks. Take some responsibility. That sort of thing."

After dinner, Charles called whom he assumed to be Roger into his study and directed him to a leather wing chair in front of his desk. Ginger sat in a slump and gazed absently out of the tall window beyond Charles's shoulder.

"There is a serious matter I have to discuss with you, my lad," said Charles with a tone of voice that implied tragic consequences. Ginger's gaze did not return to the room.

"Roger, I'm talking to you."

Ginger's eyes shifted their lazy focus from window to parent.

"Pay attention, please. This is important."

"Yeah," Ginger mumbled, eyes beginning a slow meander around the Adam-style plaster frieze.

"Do you know what adoption means?"

"Yeah."

"Good. What does it mean then?"

Silence, eyes wandering.

"Well! What *does* it mean?" Charles had not intended to raise his voice.

"What's what mean?"

"Adoption."

"Hunh?"

"Adoption. What does it mean?"

"Dunno."

"You said you did."

"Nah. I never."

"You did."

"I never."

"You did, dammit."

"Fuck off, Charlie."

For the next two years everything remained much the same in the Smythe-Halliday and Tompkins households, as if an unspoken truce had been drawn up to maintain the status quo. Penelope had taken up croquet and Charles had joined the polo club (each needing to be away from the house as much as their consciences could bear). Together, twice weekly, they visited a psychiatrist, not being at all convinced in their heart of hearts that they were not to blame for Roger's degeneration. With their solicitor's assistance, they sought to delve into his filial beginnings, hoping to absolve themselves by proving he had been a product of bad seed. These efforts were futile; the system impenetrable.

A period of sudden growth—more up than out—had turned Ginger into a gangling, loping, awkward-looking lad. The tumbling, golden curls had rearranged themselves into a shapeless straw thatch and the pretty-baby face now seemed to be continually ravaged by snarls and frowns and tough-kid grimaces. His voice was faltering, but still pitched soprano, and there wasn't a hair on his body that had not been there since the day he became Roger.

Ted, now fifteen, had grown into a big, bullocky boy with jet-black hair sprouting up hill and down dale on his muscular body; he was shaving twice a week and left several shirt buttons undone to display a broad chest showing signs of becoming as matted as his father's. Tinker, voice recently broken, was developing the same sturdy, large-boned Tompkins frame, and the sprightly tufts of black hair around cock and balls and under armpits indicated he would be, in a few more years, as hirsute as brother and dad. Tinker, less moody than Ted, was an ebullient, bright-eyed boy who had not lost his taste for cum, and now that he could, he would scoop up his own from wherever it fell to dispatch it with relish.

"Fuckin' diss-gusting," snarled Ted.

"Filthy little fucker," concurred Ginger.

"Youse both pick yer nose and eat it," scoffed Tinker, showing his cummy tongue. "Same difference," he added smugly, knowing full well his argument would go uncontested.

Ginger, without the impediments of parental supervision, carried on his daily trysts with Ted and Tinker, which now had the added zest of Tinker's ability to shoot a respectable load. A late bloomer by comparison, Ginger was still coming dry. To his secret shame, his cock, when compared with their thigh-slapping, feisty-fat poles, was a mere apology of a prick. While theirs had broad, dark brown bodies and purply-red heads poking cheekily from thick, fleshy mantles of foreskin, his small, cut cock was as insipidly pale and denuded as a skinned rabbit. And while he came not at all, Ted was delivering seven or eight generous spurts and young Tinker could let fly with four or more.

Because of the increase in height and bulk of all three boys, their routine jacking-off venue had been relocated from cramped, crawl-space quarters to the spacious attic in the garage built to house the Tompkins' cement truck. The old blankets brought there to protect naked bums from splinters and abrasions were smelly with boy sweat and encrusted with cum squirtings soaked in before Tinker could lay claim.

The day after Ginger's twelfth birthday—celebrated in the usual fashion in their attic aerie—found a morose, aimless trio without beer or cigarettes or the money to buy either. (Advised by their psychiatrist, Penelope and Charles had drastically reduced Roger's pocket money on the premise that a little personal deprivation might "bring the young fellow to his senses.")

"What'll we do this arvo?" Tinker asked.

"Dunno," said Ginger.

"Whadya feel like doin'?" Ted asked. "Wanna go to the pictures?"

"Got no money. Anyway, they've started already," Ginger said.

"What then? Play footy?" Tinker offered.

"Too bloody 'ot, ya drongo."

"Then what?"

"Climb trees?"

"Fuckin' kid's stuff," Ted sneered.

"If we had some beer an' smokes we could..."

"I told ya," Ginger snapped, "I ain't got no money."

"Don't need none," Ted chipped in.

"Don't need none?" Ginger asked warily. "How come?"

"We'll just *take* what we want. That's how come," said Ted, with a laconic half-smile.

"Pinch the stuff?" Ginger knew his friends went on regular, light-fingered forays to the local shops. Regretful that he was never invited to accompany them, he blamed his demonstrated inferiority—a gawky, chicken-chested body without muscles or hair and a twerpy, skinless dick that didn't cum—for his exclusion. "But what if we get caught?"

"We won't."

"Howdya know?" Ginger's limbs were made light by a surge of excitement.

"Done it lotsa times," sniffed blasé Ted, nodding toward Tinker for affirmation, "ain't we?"

"Yeah," chirped Tinker, all sunny smiles. "Lotsa times."

"Youse buggers comin' or ain'tcha?" Ted made a move to terminate pointless discussion.

Ginger, flattered to be asked, said flippantly, "Youse are female sheep."

For this educated observation he received a shower of sniggers from Tinker and a swift kick in the backside from Ted. "Don't get fuckin' smart-alecky with me, Fuckface."

"C'mon, less go," Tinker and Ginger voiced in unison, an octave apart.

Inside the grocery shop they fanned out and each moved down a separate aisle. Ginger's feigned nonchalance immediately attracted the attention of the owner. The Tompkins boys were well-known to him, yet their methods were so skilled he had never managed to nab them red-handed. As they strolled toward the exit, only Ginger oblivious to intense scrutiny, a box of chocolates slid down the leg of his trousers. Gold- and silver-wrapped sweets scattered like dice.

"Hey, you!" yelled the owner, sprinting toward them.

"Run," yelled Ted. And they hurled themselves at the front door. It was the entry door; it didn't budge.

They sat dejectedly on crates of lettuce in the storeroom where the owner had locked them.

"Fuckin' shit," snarled Ted, slamming his boot into the crate Ginger was sitting on.

"He'll call the cops," Tinker moaned.

"Nah, he won't."

"He will."

"He won't."

The police arrived three minutes later.

That evening, Charles called Roger into his study to review the day's events. Although the shop owner had decided not to press charges (he had tried in vain for years to gain acceptance into the polo club; Charles now personally agreed to vouch for him), the name of Smythe-Halliday would be permanently featured in the police files. When Charles's anger finally expended itself he lapsed into maudlin regret, blaming himself for Roger's errant ways. Later still, after forty minutes of contemplative and self-exonerating silence, and three tumblers of Scotch, he summoned all the cold-blooded objectivity he could muster to impress upon Roger the importance of law and order in society and the need to conduct one's life according to its rules. For the second time in his young life, Ginger heard that he must never again associate with Ted and Tinker Tompkins.

"Why not?" was the anguished cry.

"They are a bad influence."

"No, they ain't."

"They're criminals in the making."

"They ain't. They're me friends."

"They're . . . they are scum." Charles was rapidly losing his objectivity.

"They bloody ain't," Ginger shouted.

"Don't talk back. And for God's sake speak proper English."

"An' you go fuck yerself, Charlie."

During the next three years, to say no changes of great significance took place in the lives of the Smythe-Hallidays would be to disavow what time can, and often ruthlessly does, effect. Ginger did not dissociate himself from the Tompkins brothers as decreed by Charles; the happy trio continued to be as thick as the thieves they'd become. One singular, though not unexpected, development did occur that would eventually lead to, if not a cataclysmic, then certainly a dramatic turnabout in all their lives. Puberty came down on Ginger like a ton of bricks.

In a matter of a few short months, after interim years of unrelenting plainness, everything that had been perfection in the cherubic infant now returned to the pubescent youth. The ugly duckling was transformed; the body fleshed out into full-flowing, not-quite-feminine curves, the skin turned luminous and honey-gold, the straw thatch reshaped into an aureole of soft curls to frame a face of such breathtaking, androgynous beauty men and women alike were stopped in their tracks to admire or remark.

Those parts of Ginger's person to which Ted and Tinker had enjoyed intimate access over the years also underwent a radical change. His burgeoning body remained hairless except for a discreet gathering of pale, blond whorls around the stem of his cock; fluffy petals circling an overgrown stamen. Similar modest tufts peeked fetchingly out from his armpits, and the finest of fine, golden hairs decorated his long, tapering thighs and shapely calves.

Ginger's once-reticent cock now stood proudly vertical when erect, pressed authoritatively to the satiny skin of his belly, eye to winking eye with his navel. Not small, yet not grossly thick-bodied and blunt-ended like his friends' cocks (which later he would learn to describe as horsecocks), it was elegantly shaped, delicately veined and gently curved, with shaft and head in ideal proportion. When his balls ripened and descended into their plump, silken purse, a proliferation of hormones seemed to permeate every fiber of his body, driving him almost insane with fierce, lusting desires.

Ted and Tinker, always hopelessly horny, were eager and willing to gratify Ginger's newfound needs, proving to be as insatiable as he was. Their attic hideout bore witness to extended periods of exploration, experiment and carnal indulgence to near-orgiastic excess. Their afternoon get-togethers would often continue late into the evening, sometimes until the early hours of the next morning. Sometimes, at weekends, they never came down to see the light of day.

Jacking off was no longer enough for Ginger. Persuading the two brothers to allow him to suck their massive endowments posed no problems; at the first tangy taste he was addicted. Tinker's growing had caught up with Ted so when he sucked them in tandem—his favorite way—cock to cock he couldn't tell one from the other. It was Tinker's bright idea to see if he could fit the head of his dick into the pert, puckered hole between Ginger's luscious, melony asscheeks. With much maneuvering and a few false starts—Tinker huffing and puffing, Ginger giggling encouragement—a slick, probing tip eventually parted tender, pliant anal lips. Tinker couldn't manage to penetrate further, despite Ted's helpful suggestions and Ginger's begging for more. A disgruntled Ginger returned home to find—with the aid of a Tompkins-cock-sized cucumber foraged for in the pantry—that Tinker's inability to enter him fully had to do with a mere lack of lubrication rather than (his worst fear) an orifice-to-member disparity.

The next afternoon saw him ascending the attic ladder equipped with a jar of petroleum jelly and a know-it-all grin. Stripped naked and on his back in a flash, he opened his legs in a wide vee and applied gobs of Vaseline to the proposed point of entry. "Fuck me, you fools," he gurgled, stretching his milk-white buttocks apart with splayed fingers to lewdly expose his gooped-up slit. Ted flipped Tinker a quick heads or tails and Tinker, losing, sat back on his haunches to watch his big brother succeed where he'd yesterday failed.

Ted's auspicious arrival in Ginger's rectum was achieved with much bravado but little style, being altogether too fast and too sloppy. The speed was a result of unchecked, raw enthusiasm on Ted's part, and the sloppiness because of Ginger's overabundant usage of lubricant (almost half the jar, prompted by a better-to-be-sure-than-sorry rationale). Penetration complete, three sounds ensued: a short gasp of wondrous surprise from Ginger, a sigh of unexpected, intense pleasure from Ted, and a breathy exclamation of awe, "Phew," from Tinker who had scuttled between their legs, crouching low, to get a worm's-eye view of his brother's cock pistoning noisily in and out of the invitingly upturned ass.

What fascinated Tinker even more than observing at close range the three or four slimy inches of cockshaft appearing from and disappearing back into the elastic sphincter ring, was the rhythmic gyration of Ted's huge, low-hanging balls. Unable to resist a need to confirm their weightiness, he reached forward and cupped them loosely, letting them perform their voluptuous dance on his open palm (two double-yolkers flopping heavily in a crinkly-soft, leather sack). Meanwhile, Ginger's tight, virgin asshole, clutching Ted's cock like a fiery fist, was bringing him fast toward climax. The titillation of his balls was the last straw; he grunted, thrust deeply, and unloaded his ten squirts of semen ten inches inside Ginger's rectum.

"That was the fuckin' greatest," Ted panted as he withdrew.

"Now me." Tinker was already taking Ted's place between once-innocent, outstretched thighs. The sight of creamy juices flowing from the gaping asslips caused him a moment's hesitation, but resisting the temptation to suck up the oozing disharge, he positioned his cock and plunged himself to the hilt in one inconsiderate thrust. Arriving where he'd never been before, experiencing for the first time all the intricacies and indescribables of ass-fucking, Tinker's excitement was so high-pitched that he flooded into Ginger immediately.

"Aw, Rog, can I have another go in a bit?" he asked, droopy-mouthed, squeezing the last few drops from the tip of his cock with thumb and finger and ferrying the morsel to his tongue.

"We'll see," replied Ginger. He tried to sound noncommittal, but his eyes revealed his own disappointment that Tinker had shot his load so soon.

Thrilled by these new and wonderful sensations of pleasurable fullness, of rhythmic massaging deep inside his body, of being utterly possessed, Ginger knew that fucking was what he was made for, that all the inconsistencies and adversities he had endured were simply preparing him, physically, mentally, emotionally, to be an exquisite receptacle for the male penis. Prostrate on his back with his long legs hooked over powerful shoulders, with fuck-hungry, young stallions straining their hard, muscular bodies against his, urgently pounding their huge cocks into his yearning bowels, filling him with their potent maleness, *that* was where he belonged. *That* was who he was.

That evening, Ted and Tinker twice took turns to thoroughly complete Ginger's deflowering (he came on his belly each time they came inside). Ginger, refreshed and revivified by several swigs of bitter ale—his latent talents now out in the open and reasoning that once the cat is out of the bag it's pointless to pretend it was ever in it—challenged his friends to fuck more creatively:

"Wanna see if youse can both do me at the same time?"

The Tompkins boys, not about to miss an opportunity to have their dicks again so deliciously accommodated, accepted the challenge without knowing how to meet it. Ginger knew how; he was full of ideas. To him the possibilities of coupling cocks and asses seemed limited only by a paucity of imagination. Determination more than good intentions, he realized, was what was required to accomplish the goal, so he took charge, became assertive. He positioned Tinker, dubious but not resisting, on his back on the blankers. He straddled his waist and guided the upstanding cock between poised, pallid asscheeks. He descended, feeling his hole nudged, prodded and harmoniously entered. With an exclamation of delight, he pressed his buttocks conclusively to Tinker's groin, glutting himself with the meaty, ten-inch member.

They rotated their joined hips to lodge the cock as deeply as possible, then Ginger bent forward, sprawling his upper body across Tinker, torso to torso. He tilted his buttocks carefully—keeping the cock fully embedded—to present his plugged asshole for sacrifice. Seeing this obscene offering, believing two cocks in one hole just might be possible, Ted gripped his and knee-walked between layered legs, aiming its drooling head at the base of his buried brother's. Ginger, experiencing a sudden, stabbing pain, bit his bottom lip and slowly circled his rump; each inch by penetrating inch was both pleasurable and painful.

"You okay?" Ted asked, loving the constriction but anatomically unsure of Ginger's ability to accept the combined mass of two already-overlarge cocks.

"Hmmm... it's great," purred Ginger. "But go real easy."

Not able to assist in a practical way, Tinker licked the trickling sweat from Ginger's arched neck and enjoyed the curious sensation of having his big brother's cock and his sliding belly to belly. When Ted was shoved in as far as he could go (three sets of balls bunched as tightly as coconuts), he paused there at Ginger's cautioning request: "Hold still a bit till I get used to it."

"It's like having yer dick in a vice," Tinker chuckled, "a nice vice, but."

"Sure yer okay?" Ted asked heedfully. It was incomprehensible to him that this slender-hipped kid could so readily house what was as big as his forearm.

"Yeah... Oh, yeah..." crooned Ginger. "Fuck me now... but do it real slow."

Ted tried to fuck as slowly as he could but the tension built quickly to unbearable; he knew he was fucking faster than he should. Tinker could do nothing to facilitate the fuck so he held on to Ginger, moistening smooth flesh with heated breaths, while his brother's clamped cock slid hotly up and down the length of his own. Ginger exulted in each long, plunging thrust; the pain of the double breaching long since gone.

Excitement expanded rapidly to overtake and consume the cock-connected bodies. Ginger felt Tinker's limbs lock rigid around him for his shuddering climax. The gushing, warm fluids lubricated the two-in-one cock and this sudden new slippage was all that was needed to set off Ted's explosion. Ginger, too, let fly a quick succession of creamy spurts to matt Tinker's flourishing chest.

Later, when he saw they were out-and-out sated, Ginger carefully stowed the Tompkins boys' wilted, sticky cocks into their raggedy trousers, buttoned them up (this service, he cautioned himself, could become habit-forming), and set off, reluctantly, for home.

In the months that followed Ginger's remarkable maturescence, both Ted and Tinker—now fucking him routinely every afternoon—developed a leech-like possessiveness, a shameless craving, a seemingly unquenchable passion for his physical charms and blatant sexuality. Ted, recently turned eighteen, had become so utterly infatuated by his sensual beauty and unbridled eroticism, he broke off his engagement to a neighborhood girl.

"Rog, baby, fuckin' you is so much better," was his hoarse-whispered reason as he gratefully sank his swollen cock into Ginger's delectable, cloying asshole.

They nurtured his vanity, He fed on their adulation. And as they adored him, as they fawned over him, he grew self-confident and his ego expanded. His vanity, as it increased, brought a note of strain to his naturally frank face. There was a tension that had not previously existed. And so their relationship, little by little, altered. Because they were so much in awe of him, so fervidly desiring and needing to possess him, he began to loathe them. He began to see them as Penelope and Charles saw them; as Roger would see them.

Ginger devised a clever scheme to correct the awkward imbalance in his life. After school one afternoon, while walking with Ted and Tinker through an arcade of exclusive shops (not accidentally but at his suggestion), he stopped them dead in their tracks in front of a jeweler's display window.

"Get an eyeful of that," he said, pointing to a diamond brooch in the shape of a swan; its single eye a ruby, its beak three amethysts.

"My mum would go fer that," he added, covetously.

"So'd mine," agreed Tinker. Ted whistled his agreement thorugh his teeth.

"Why dontcha give t'er then?" Ginger said with cool and cunning calm.

"Bet the fucker costs thousands," Ted scowled.

"Since when does *that* give us any worries?" prompted Ginger, smiling snidely.

"Jees, you mean..." Tinker's mouth sagged open.

"Take it," said Ginger.

"They'd send us to jail... or a 'ome... if we got caught."

"So? Who's gunna get caught?" Ginger laughed mockingly. "Yer just scared."

"I ain't," snapped Tinker.

"Fuckin' scared," taunted Ginger. "Nothin' happened before when we got caught. Nothin'd happen again. 'Cept this time we ain't gunna."

"But... if..." Tinker was still skeptical.

"Fuck the ifs and buts. Ain't ya ever heard of makin' plans?"

"Yeah, but still..."

"Shaddup and listen." Ginger walked them out of the arcade, outlining his strategy for the law-proof acquisition of the glittering prize. His guile, persuasion and invidious charm were lethal, making mincemeat out of Ted's indifference and Tinker's feeble protestations.

At dusk, an hour after the shops had closed, the three boys came sauntering down the empty arcade. Ted held the brick in his right hand, newspaper-wrapped in the disguise of fish and chips. They ambled past the display window three times, glancing about furtively, then, when Ginger hissed "Now," Ted hurled the package at the glass. The noise, immense in the unsuspecting twilight, was immediately reinforced by a wailing alarm over the shop door. Ted reached into the debris and gingerly extracted the brooch. The trio, whooping with cries of victory and nervous release, sprinted swiftly through the echoing arcade and turned the corner into the street where they were confronted by two policemen.

When the two young thieves and their unwitting accomplice appeared in court ten days later, it was Roger Charles Whittington Smythe-Halliday, not Ginger, who stood so serenely before the judge. Standing poised and immaculate in a three-piece gray flannel suit, he listened respectfully as his involvement in the crime was sadly lamented at length, then summarily dismissed as a clear case of innocence corrupted (Charles having pulled strings at the club in addition to hiring the best legal counsel money could buy, as Roger well knew he would). There was no fine, no probation, no admonishment; he walked away scot-free, the embodiment of good breeding and upper-middle-class values, to an accompanying chorus of sympathetic clucks and ever-so-understanding smiles.

Ted and Tinker, on the books as frequent offenders, were promptly dispatched to a juvenile correctional institution until such time as the court deemed them suitably rehabilitated to rejoin society.

In the taxi, coming home from court, Penelope and Charles were not at all sure how to respond to Roger, who kept up a steady stream of agreeable (and grammatically correct) conversation, pleasantly peppered with phrases such as:

"Daddy, how splendid of you to . . ." and ". . . what a divine hat, Mummy dearest."

While inwardly rejoicing, they were concerned that the incarceration of his childhood friends might cause him to lapse into a homicidal depression, or worse still, become verbally or even physically abusive. Penelope, trying to broach this delicate issue, made sentimental and oblique reference to the tragedy of staunch friends cruelly parted.

"Oh, *them*," Roger grimaced, and with a sweet smile of condescension, said, "Good riddance to bad rubbish."

At home, Roger politely excused himself to go to his room

to change clothes and "clear out all that dreadful old junk" from his toy cupboard. He was planning to spend a quiet evening at home, he told them, and was so very much looking forward to dining, *en famille.* He bowed graciously from the room.

When the dinner gong sounded some hours later, Penelope and Charles were passing through the entry hall at the exact moment Roger began his descent on the curving staircase. They stopped, transfixed, as as vision of loveliness swept down toward them. The beautiful, willowy figure, clad in a fluttering gown of pure white silk, greeted them with perfect lips shaping a radiant smile of such warmth and devotion that they knew at once this was the child for whom, all these years, they had secretly longed—their darling daughter. Miss Ginger Roger.

How Donny Connor Got His Condom

ONE MONDAY MORNING after her son Donald had gone to school, Nora Connor found a condom in the top drawer of his wardrobe. She was not snooping, but checking to see if he had enough clean underwear for the week. She carried it downstairs in the palm of her hand to show it to her husband Nigel Connor, Donald's father.

"Look," she said. "Look what I found in Donny's room."

"What," he said. Nigel Connor put aside the *Sydney Morning Herald* and set down the spoon he was using to stir sugar into his tea.

"Look," she repeated. "It was under his underpants."

"What is it?" He had not removed his reading glasses so all he saw in his wife's outstretched hand was a glossy red and gold blur.

"It's . . . it's a prophylactic."

"It is? Hmmm."

"Well, what are we going to do about it?"

"What do you *want* to do?" Nigel Connor picked up the spoon and resumed stirring his tea.

"I think you should talk to him."

"What about?"

"About . . . about, you know. About *these* things." Nora Connor held up the small square packet economically between thumb and finger tips, and shook it like a little bell. "Explain what they're for."

"If he's got one it's a dead cert he knows what they're for."

"I still think you should *talk* to him. It's a father's responsibility."

"I wouldn't know what to say."

"Didn't your father tell you about sex and things?"

"My old man? Hell, no!"

"Well, how did you find out?"

"Same as Donny, most likely. From other boys at school."

"That's awful. It's our duty as parents to . . . to . . ." Her voice trailed away as it occurred to her that if she pressed the matter too vehemently the task of performing the duty might fall to her. A new and alarming thought suddenly entered her mind.

"What if he's *using* them?"

Her husband sipped his tea, thoughtfully. "Then we don't need to tell him how to, do we?" he said. And picked up the morning paper, shaking it to uncrease the pages.

* * *

I *WAS* USING THEM.

I am Nora and Nigel Connor's son, Donald Henry Connor, and that day—the day of Mum's earth-shattering discovery—I was approximately fourteen years, three months and one week old. To say I was using them is not the exact truth; rather my friend Roderick Matthews was using them. That he was using them in the manner for which they were intended is also a moot point; at that time, that particular Monday morning, it was not at all clear to me what their precise function was. I did know they were designed to be worn, glove-like, on the erect penis. I knew this because I had seen it happen with my own eyes just one week before.

The previous Monday, I'd seen Roderick Matthews, the person I admired most in the entire world, wearing one. While I secretly watched, he had carefully unrolled a translucent, skin-tight tube onto his incredibly huge cock and did something very peculiar and interesting to cute, little Dicky Appleton. The occasion of that first sighting is burned into my memory, as vividly unforgettable as images caught on a movie screen, retained in every detail.

Roderick Matthews, the only child of a glamorous, socialite mother and a father who conducts non-specific business internationally, lives in a luxury block of flats overlooking Lavender Bay, while the rest of us have to make do with boring parents in boring houses. Save for his mother, who alone calls him Roderick, and his father and the teachers at school who call him Rod, he is known to the rest of us as Rodder. A sun-bronzed, burly boy, six feet tall, handsome in a roughshod way with a beautiful head of black, curly hair, Rodder is pursued endlessly. He is undoubtedly the most popular boy at school, and he is in my class.

Even though Rodder is almost three years older than I, easily eight inches taller, and sports an abundance of body hair and muscles where few of us have much of either, we are in the same class because he has no aptitude for applying his mind. Applying his body is where he shines. He is a wizard at sports, especially football, and is additionally the best marble player in the whole school; the unbeaten champion. His outstanding achievements on the football field, impressive more for their brutish physicality than finesse, give him stature and eminence among his peers, and his prowess at marbles incites slack-mouthed, tongue-lolling adulation from the younger boys.

Rodder, absorbing hero-worship as if it is his birthright, is good-natured, well-mannered, and magnanimously bighearted as befits the wealthy. When he speaks, which he rarely does, his voice is manly-deep and spine-tingling. Known for physical triumphs and few words, he has foxy eyes and a foxier mind. But more notably, he has a particular fondness for ravaging the rectums of his adoring, young fans. I discovered Rodder's unusual penchant that Monday when I followed my boyhood intuition and played sleuth after school.

As usual, there had been cigarette smoking behind the incinerators and a game of marbles which Rodder had easily won. As our raggle-taggle group disbanded, I overheard him offer to teach Dicky Appleton the special maneuver he'd employed to win the game if he would wait until they were alone. I pricked up my ears. There was something about the inflection in his voice, a hint of prurient entreaty, and his smile had a distinctly lascivious upturn at the corners. Without a doubt something suspicious was afoot.

Dicky Appleton accepted the offer wih a vigorous nodding of his head and beamed from ear to ear, his gleaming white

of the boy's buttocks and spat copiously into the crevice. Warm saliva flowed over Dicky's tender ass crack. He dropped his marble and jerked his head over his shoulder, a look of utter disbelief on his angelic face. As understanding seeped into his mind, his expression changed to horror and he gyrated his body to escape. But escape was impossible, his struggles ineffectual. Rodder's big hands were on the boy's bony shoulders, pinning his upper body uselessly to the ground as the head of his cock pressed into the slickened anal opening.

Dicky cried out, a pitiful scream, and again tried to struggle free, but he was locked in a viselike grip, weighted into the dry grass. I thought of an innocent lamb fallen prey to a ravenous wolf as Rodder's huge cock thrust urgently between the boy's delicate, melon-shaped buttocks and quickly disappeared from sight. Rodder was an accomplished seducer, however, not at all a rampaging animal. Lowering his powerful body carefully across Dicky, he stroked his hair in a loving way, nuzzled his neck and mouthed breathy, sweet nothings in his ear. Amorous entreaties, I wondered, or promises of more marbles? Whatever the case, Dicky sobbings soon subsided and he resigned himself to his ravishment without further protest or complaint.

From my hiding place I watched the undulating rise and fall of Rodder's taut buttocks, catching glimpses of his cock moving in and out like a steam-driven piston, trying to imagine how it woulid feel to have all that hard flesh pushing inside you. I undid my zipper and released my cock, gripping it in my fist and masturbating it to the same rhythm as Rodder's thrusting hips. Dicky's eyes were still wet with tears and he looked dazed, slightly bewildered, but he certainly did not appear to be suffering distress or discomfort. My asshole twitched; I felt certain it had to be a good feeling. I envied Dicky Appleton. I wanted a cock inside me, Rodder's huge cock. I pushed my finger into my ass imagining it to be his cock, to have his thickness. I poked it in as far as it would go, then pulled it out and pushed it back in, out and in, again and again as fast as I could. And my cock exploded.

As my cum jetted into the grass, I heard Rodder groan. His

exact place Dicky had occupied and slipped the dribbling cocoon over two bunched fingers and a thumb. With surprisingly little effort I inserted them, sheathed as Rodder's cock had been sheathed, into my hungry ass. Making the motions of a cock fucking, I wanked my dick in my other hand to the same tempo. I pushed in deeply as I came, vowing that one day in the near future it would be Rodder's big, hard cock pushing in there instead.

That was easier vowed than done. Rodder, although monosyllabically polite to my face, demonstrated no noticeable enthusiasm for my rear end. Despite the fact that I began wearing an old pair of threadbare and skintight shorts to school and edged in front of him at every available opportunity to present him with a creditable rendition of Marilyn Monroe's ass-wigging walk from *Niagara,* he remained charmingly indifferent. Not so Mr. Mainwaring, our headmaster, who collared me between classes in the corridor.

"This is the second day in a row you've worn those things, Connor. Personal hygiene and pride in one's appearance aside, they are outgrown to the point of obscenity. I can't believe your parents let you out of the door looking like that."

My mother certainly would not have (I changed into the garment in question in the school dunny before the bell), although my parents and I have developed, over the years, a tacit policy of non-involvement. This has proven to create a happier home life for all concerned. As I never have any personal conversations with them, loving them is easy, and free of guilt-edged obligations, they return my love with equal generosity. A total lack of communication, I firmly believe, is the root of a totally harmonious family.

My inability to arouse Rodder's interest coupled with Mr. Mainwaring's curt admonishment made me intensely depressed. For the fourth time in my life, I contemplated suicide. The other occasions, in comparison, seemed mere trifles: jeans back from the laundry that had not shrunk, my address book mislaid, a haircut with way too much off the back and sides; all not out of the ordinary, spur-of-the-moment incitements to self-destruct.

Trying to look at the situation objectively, applying myself with some positive thinking, it occurred to me that Dicky Appleton had won the day by losing on the battlefield; the conquered had captured the spoils. On Thursday morning before school, I emptied my china koala money box and purchased two glassies, two alleys, two connies, and a genuine agate shooter, challenging Rodder to a game of marbles I knew I couldn't possibly win. When he asked what the stakes were, I looked him fair and square in his smoldering, ink-black eyes and said, quoting from what I thought was Shakespeare, "Use me as you will."

After the match, happily vanquished, I lay back invitingly in the grass and gave him a self-sacrificing smile. "At your service," I proffered, kittenishly.

Rodder gave me a good-humored rabbit-punch and ordered me across to the corner shop to buy him cigarettes. Nursing the humiliation of my now bitter defeat, I sauntered homeward, licking my wounds and rethinking my modus operandi. All week I'd employed devious strategies to attract his special attention, and all had failed. As too much serious thought gives me a headache, I looked to my boyhood intuition for guidance. I was told that it was high time I used a more direct approach. I was reminded that tomorrow, being Friday, there would be an after-school football game. It was pointed out to me that after the game two virile male bodies, aroused by blood sport, emotionally charged and unclothed in the shower room, would surely couple spontaneously.

Being only a linesman I seldom get dirty or need to shower after a game, but I did that day. Still dripping wet, I struggled through his clamoring throng of admirers to tell Rodder I urgently needed his help in a rather personal matter. The well-brought-up boy he was, he dismissed his entourage, seeming especially regretful to see baby-faced Reggie Ward's chubby buttocks disappearing through the steam.

"What can I do for you?" he asked, with a bemused smile.

I stepped as closely as I dared—us both being naked save for skimpy towels wrapped loosely around hips—and released my breath. "Do me like you did Dicky Appleton on Monday."

Rodder registered no surprise, not even a flicker of surprise; he didn't bat an eyelid. "Donny, old chap," he said, as soberly solicitous as my father. "You're an okay bloke. Y'know, nice-looking an' all that. But ya gotta unnerstand, it's the young-uns I fancy. No hard feelings. Okay?"

No hard feelings! Everying *but* my feelings was hard. Close proximity to the sweaty panorama of his gorgeous body—mountains and valleys of tanned, muscular flesh—had caused an immediate erection, scarcely contained by the scant drape of my towel. My boyhood intuition screamed for drastic measures. Throwing caution to the wind and my towel to the floor, I burst into tears.

Several seconds of palpable stillness elapsed, which I sobbed through with some difficulty. I was beginning to consider raising my head to see if, in fact, he was still in the room, when I felt the sudden warmth of strong hands on my shoulders. Taking that as my cue, I let all the strength escape from my body and collapsed gratefully into his unwitting embrace. As I'd hoped, a distraught and supplicating body in intimate contact with his own was enough to desensitize all objective perception and activate a multitude of erotic responses. Which is a polite way of saying Rodder was altogether too horny to resist an opportunity for a fast fuck when it was literally dumped in his lap.

To coinciding gasps of mutual amazement, he brought me down with him to the wet, tiled floor, splaying out my willing, rag-doll limbs and smothering my throat with lusting kisses. His intentions, fortunately, were entirely dishonorable; he needed to bring his primed weapon home to the hilt as soon as possible. Without affording me the time to experience all the subtle details of the process, he positioned himself over me like a predatory animal. With one hand under my buttocks and the other firmly grasping his manhood, he adjusted the tilts and angles to align his sword with my scabbard. Bold but gentle, as any well-bred knight would be, he entered to give succor and comfort to his damsel (me, in this case) in distress.

Accommodating Rodder's monstrous cock wasn't a classic

hot-knife-into-butter penetration; the pain more closely resembled a hot-knife-into-me stabbing. I did not cry out, though my teeth on his shoulder drew blood. Searing and intense, the pain was gradually replaced by less precise, more vaporous sensations of gratification and well-being; there was a satisfying feeling of fullness along with a prideful sense of accomplishment. My body relaxed and expanded and flowed into his. He crooned soothing words of deep pleasure and endearment and I succumbed to him completely, accepting his entire shaft with consummate ease.

Rodder's magnificent cock, now stuffed deeply inside me, was even more wonderful than I'd imagined. Its slow frictioning movements sent ripples of raw pleasure throughout my body; nerve endings everywhere became vibrantly alive. I sucked and nipped his hardened nipples and kissed his wet flesh wherever I could, reveling in the sensory slickness of worked muscles and fresh sweat. Breathing was heavier, his and mine, and there were contented moans interspersed with croaked whispers of pleading and approval.

"Mmmm . . . gimme it big Rodder," I hummed. "Gimme all that big cock."

His long, rhythmic strokes were determined and constant. I countered with my ass muscles, clenching and releasing, to parry his thrusts.

"Donny . . . Oh, Donny . . . it's so good," he gasped. "So good in there . . . so good . . . an' so hot."

It was all over too soon. With a bellowing cry, repeating as an anguished echo around the tiled walls, he plunged his bursting cock to the ultimate depths of my upthrust ass. Grunting like a rutted pig, he emptied his load inside me, collapsing his full body weight into me, choking for air. I kept him deeply entrenched, holding his rock-hard buttocks until his ordeal was over; as his ejaculation subsided his asscheeks unclenched.

Recovering his breath, Rodder then did to me precisely what he'd done to Dicky after their fuck. Spreading my legs, he scrambled between them and pounced on my aching prick, swallowing it whole with avaricious glee. Already simmering on the verge of orgasm, I came instantly, squirting my cum into his massaging throat.

"Phew, I'm all sweaty again," grinned Rodder, giving his fruity lips a thorough licking, then wiping them with the back of his hand. "Let's hop in the same stall so's we can soap each other up." Under the spray we were immediately skittish, lathering playfully and laughing like loonies, rubbing our soapy bodies suggestively against one another, tickling our particulars and diddling our dicks. "Grrr," I growled, gnawing up and down the meaty length of his cock. "I'm a poor, half-starved puppy that needs a bone." Mottled with suds, I crawled out of the shower with Rodder slavering at my tail, pretending I was his bitch dog in heat, sniffing and tongue-wiping my ass. "Bow wow," he barked, a Great Danish basso, "I'll give ya a hot, juicy bone." I braced myself on all fours; he mounted from the rear (his bark not worse than his bite). "Woof woof," I urged over my shoulder, raising my rump, "feed me that big, doggie dick." With one hefty shove it slurped easily in, my channel well-lubricated by his previous cumming. "Grrr, grrr," I growled, happily, getting my second Rodder fuck.

He fucked me three times, right there and then on the scummy tiles, that Friday afternoon. To inhibit our ravening lust, we agreed to take our fourth shower in separate stalls, for fear that we'd die of waterlogged fucking. While toweling down and dressing, Rodder was more verbally expressive than he'd ever been. He enthusiastically admitted what while the fucking had obviously been first-time fabulous and mind-blowing for me, it had been equally so for him. The "young-uns" it seemed, though preferred up till then, were passive partners: pretty, little take-it-as-it-comes fellows with dewy-fresh asses to fuck, but all take and no give; just one-way streets with no grist for the mill; no reciprocal jousting up their sleeves. Rodder's metaphors might have been a mess, but I knew what he meant; I'd given him a run for his money.

I might have been a novice, a starry-eyed ingenue, but when it came to my first big performance, I more than rose to the occasion. I was a diva, a fully-fledged prima donna, a virtuoso player. A fucking natural. I take flattery well; I dropped to my knees humbly and fumbled for a thanksgiving toot on his organ.

"Um, Donny, old chap. If ya don't mind, I'm done in, for today," he explained politely, extricating his limp cock from my slobbering lips. "Next time, I'll let ya have a good suck before we fuck," he added, seeing the disappointment in my upturned face.

"When's that?"

"How's tomorrow?"

"No good," I grimaced, "my parents are taking me camping down the coast for the weekend."

Rodder's brow wrinkled as he made his mind work more than it cared to. "Um, how about Friday?" he grinned, his brainwave making his black eyes sparkle. "After school. At my place. An' ya can stay till Monday."

"What about them?" I asked, with regard to his parents.

"They'll be gone."

"Where to?"

"Um, not sure. London, I think. No, maybe it's Rome."

"Okay. Till then, can I keep it?"

"Keep what?"

"Y'know. *It.* The thing you wore for Dicky on Monday, but didn't today."

Rodder chuckled and gave me a rabbit-punch. "I would've, but I never got a chance to put it on, did I? Never seen such a cock-hungry young bugger as you," he said, cupping my crotch with one hand and squeezing my asscheeks with the other.

"Well, can I?" I wriggled my bottom appreciatively, but I was determined not to be sidetracked.

"Okay. But only till Friday." He took a bright red and gold packet out of his pocket and handed it to me.

"Why only till then?" I asked, gingerly accepting the packet and pocketing it covetously.

"Coz Friday we'll need it," he grinned wickedly, slipping his hand up the leg of my shorts, finding and fingering my crack. "Friday, I'll put it on me dick, then I'll put me dick up there (pushing his finger inside me), an' we'll fuck like rabbits all weekend."

Warm shivers of anticipation thickened my cock. Knowing we had a whole week to wait, a new thought occurred to me. Pushing down to take more of his finger, I said, flirtatiously, "And no more doing it with Dicky. Or Reggie Ward. Or anyone else."

"Aw, Donny, but . . ."

"No more," I insisted, and bore possessively down to take all of his probing finger into my ass. "Promise?"

"Aw . . ."

"Promise?"

"I promise."

* * *

ON MONDAY MORNING, when Nora Connor saw that her husband Nigel had finished his third cup of tea and the sports section of the newspaper, she picked up the brightly packaged condom from the lid of the marmalade jar where it had been put to rest while its fate was decided.

"So, what are we going to do about this?" she asked her husband, holding the packet distastefully at arm's length.

"Hmmm?" Nigel Connor folded his reading glasses and carefully collapsed the paper.

"This! This *thing* of Donny's." Nora brought the condom to within six inches of Nigel's nose and dangled it, pointedly.

"Well, it's *his* isn't it?"

"Yes, but . . ."

"So, put it back."

"Back!"

"Yes, back in the drawer where you found it."

"But . . . but, why?"

"Its a dead cert he's going to need it."

AIDS RISK REDUCTION GUIDELINES FOR HEALTHIER SEX

As given by Bay Area Physicians for Human Rights and reprinted from *In the Heat of Passion: How to Have Hotter, Safer Sex.*

NO RISK. *Most of these activities involve only skin-to-skin contact, thereby avoiding exposure to blood, semen, and vaginal secretions. This assumes there are no breaks in the skin.* **1) Social kissing** (dry). **2) Body massage, hugging. 3) Body to body rubbing** (frottage). **4) Light S&M** (without bruising or bleeding). **5) Using one's own sex toys. 6) Mutual masturbation** (male or external female). Care should be taken to avoid exposing the partners to ejaculate or vaginal secretions. Seminal, vaginal and salivary fluids should not be used as lubricants.

LOW RISK. *In these activities small amounts of certain body fluids might be exchanged, or the protective barrier might break causing some risk.* **1) Anal or vaginal intercourse with condom.** Risk is incurred if the condom breaks or if semen spills into the rectum or vagina. The risk is further reduced if one withdraws before climax. **2) Fellatio interruptus** (sucking, stopping before climax). Pre-ejaculate fluid may contain HIV. Saliva may contain HIV in low concentration. The insertive partner should warn the receptive partner before climax to prevent exposure to a large volume of semen. If mouth or genital sores are present, risk is increased. Likewise, action which causes mouth or genital injury will increase risk. **3) Fellatio with condom** (sucking with condom). Risk is low unless breakage occurs. **4) Mouth-to-mouth kissing** (French kissing, wet kissing). HIV is present in saliva in such low concentration that salivary exchange is unlikely to transmit the virus. Risk is increased if sores in the mouth or bleeding gums are present. **5) Oral-vaginal or oral-anal contact with protective barrier,** e.g. a latex dam, obtainable through a dental supply house. Do not reuse latex barrier. **6) Manual anal contact with glove** (fisting with glove). If the glove does not break, virus transmission should not occur. However, significant trauma can still be inflicted on the rectal tissues leading to other medical problems. **7) Manual vaginal contact with glove** (internal). See above.

MODERATE RISK. *These activities involve tissue trauma and/or exchange of body fluids which may transmit HIV or other sexually transmitted disease.* **1) Fellatio** (sucking to climax). Semen may contain high concentrations of HIV and if absorbed through open sores in the mouth or digestive tract could pose risk. **2) Oral-anal contact** (rimming). HIV may be contained in blood-contaminated feces or in the anal rectal lining. This practice also poses high risk of transmission of parasites and other gastrointestinal infections. **3) Cunnilingus** (oral-vaginal contact). Vaginal secretions and menstrual blood have been shown to harbor HIV, thereby causing risk to the oral partner if open lesions are present in the mouth or digestive tract. **4) Manual rectal contact** (fisting). Studies have indicated a direct association between fisting and HIV infection for both partners. This association may be due to concurrent use of recreational drugs, bleeding, pre-fisting semen exposure, or anal intercourse with ejaculation. **5) Sharing sex toys. 6) Ingestion of urine.** HIV has not been shown to be transmitted via urine; however, other immunosuppressive agents or infections may be transmitted in this manner.

HIGH RISK. *These activities have been shown to transmit HIV.* **1) Receptive anal intercourse without condom.** All studies imply that this activity carries the highest risk of transmitting HIV. **2) Insertive anal intercourse without condom.** Studies suggest that men who participate only in this activity are at less risk of being infected than their partners who are rectally receptive; however the risk is still significant. It carries high risk of infection by other sexually transmitted diseases. **3) Vaginal intercourse without condom.**

Sex is an important part of our lives. We owe it to ourselves and to our partners to keep it as healthy (low risk) as we can.

BOOKS FROM LEYLAND PUBLICATIONS/G.S. PRESS

- ☐ **MEATMEN** Volume 4. Large-sized collection of gay comics: Tom of Finland, Stephen etc. $12.95. [Also: **MEATMEN** Vols. 2 & 3: $12.95 each.]
- ☐ **OH BOY!** Sex Comics by Brad Parker. $11.95.
- ☐ **YOUNG NUMBERS and Other True Gay Encounters** Vol. 4. 200 pp. of hot male-male sex stories. $11.00.
- ☐ **HUMONGOUS: True Gay Encounters** Volume 5. $11.00. [Also: **LUST/HARD/MANPLAY: True Gay Encounters** Vols. 1, 2, 3: $11.00 each.]
- ☐ **HOT ACTS/ORGASMS/HOT STUDS/SINGLEHANDED/ WHEN I WAS 18: Homosexual Encounters from *First Hand*** Vols. 1–5. $11.95 each (or $55.55 for all five volumes).
- ☐ **HEADSTOPS: True Revelations & Strange Happenings from *18 Wheeler,*** Vol. 4. $11.95. Encounters with truckers. [Also: **TRASH/TRUCKER/SEXSTOP** (3 vols.). $11.95 each.]
- ☐ **MEAT/FLESH/SEX/CUM/JUICE/WADS/CREAM.** Best-selling **True Homosexual Experiences from *S.T.H.*** Edited by Boyd McDonald (7 vols.). $13.00 each (or $85.55 for all seven.)
- ☐ **CUT/UNCUT: True Gay Experiences of Foreskin & Circumcision.** Illustrated. $11.00.
- ☐ **STAND BY YOUR MAN and Other One-Handed, Two-Fisted Stories** by Jack Fritscher. $11.00.
- ☐ **DRUM BEATS: Walt Whitman's Civil War Boy Lovers.** Letters to Walt Whitman from young Civil War soldier boyfriends. $10.95. [Also: **CALAMUS LOVERS: Walt Whitman's Working-Class Camerados.** $10.95.] Both edited by Charley Shively.
- ☐ **IN THE HEAT OF PASSION: How to Have Hotter, Safer Sex,** by Richard Locke. Complete illustrated guide. Special discount price $1.95.
- ☐ **THE DELIGHT OF HEARTS.** Stories of boy prostitutes etc. in ancient Araby by Ahmad al-Tifashi. Trans. by E. A. Lacey. $11.00.
- ☐ **AUSSIE BOYS/AUSSIE HOT.** Gay Encounters from Australia by Rusty Winter. $11.00 each volume.
- ☐ **SURFER SEX.** By Rusty Winter. $8.95.

TO ORDER: Check books wanted (or list them on a separate sheet) and send check/money order to Leyland Publications, P.O. Box 40397, San Francisco, CA 94140. **Postage included in prices quoted.** Calif. residents add 6½% sales tax. Mailed in unmarked book envelopes. Add $1 for complete catalogue.